W9-ANP-562

My Last Summer with You:
no fanfare for a withered rose.

By

Fidelis O. Mkparu

WITHDRAWN
FROM THE RODMAN PUBLIC LIBRARY

RODMAN PUBLIC LIBRARY

38212002967450
Main Adult Fiction
Mkparu, F
Mkparu, Fidelis O
My last summer with you

© 2012 Fidelis O. Mkparu
All Rights Reserved.

No part of this publication may be reproduced, stored in a retrieval system, or transmitted, in any form or by any means, electronic, mechanical, photocopying, recording, or otherwise, without the written permission of the author.

First published by Dog Ear Publishing
4010 W. 86th Street, Ste H
Indianapolis, IN 46268
www.dogearpublishing.net

ISBN: 978-1-4575-1258-2

This book is printed on acid-free paper.

This book is a work of fiction. Places, events, and situations in this book are purely fictional and any resemblance to actual persons, living or dead, is coincidental.

Printed in the United States of America

Acknowledgement

Front cover concept and art
by my special friend Rosie Smith

Dedication

To my dad who possessed great savoir-faire, and my mom who mastered the art of perseverance. To Oby for understanding and accepting me with all my limitations.

Monday, December 6, 2010

Chapter 1

I t was a very cold windy winter day. I was sitting in my warm office listening to whistling sounds made by trees stripped lifeless by autumn weather as they were whipped by the cold torturous winter wind. I chose to imagine, rather than feel the effect of such cold wind on my aging joints. As the cold wind picked up speed, the subdued trees wailed with higher pitch. I looked at my watch to confirm the inevitable; it was time for me to go out for a needed lunch.

Although my stomach was protesting loudly for sustenance, I could not find the courage to venture out. I stood up from my chair and walked to the window to convince myself that I was no match for the lashing effect of a brutal cold winter wind. The sky was covered by dreary dark clouds, and the tree branches were flagellated by the cold wind that seemed to change direction every second. I was unequivocally convinced that staying indoors was my best choice. I cursed my aging body, which I felt could not fare well if exposed to such a cruel unforgiving sub-zero **w**inter day. Unrelenting cold wind succeeded in holding me captive inside my office.

When the rebelling sounds from my stomach became louder than the outside wind, I decided to have tea and crackers which were available. All I wanted was something to quiet the annoying accusatory sounds from my stomach. As I sat down, waiting for my tea to boil, I drifted into a daydream. I had flashes of the last rainy summer when blooming flowers defied season. Images of fresh roses that bloomed in my garden flashed before me. I drifted to grass fields of my childhood, where butterflies perched with fanning wings, grasshoppers jumps were propelled by their hind legs, and the afternoon sun titillated my brown skin.

"Sir, you have a telephone call." It was my secretary calling my attention to a blinking telephone line.

My electric teapot was percolating, and the cold wind was still blowing when I reluctantly returned to reality. I picked up the receiver, aware that I would be delayed for a lunch break I deserved. "Hello, may I help you?" My voice was probably hurried.

"Yes, you can help me, Joseph." The caller sounded excited, but I could not place the voice. Her voice sounded euphonious, but she did not find it necessary to introduce herself. She carried on as if we were close friends having a routine conversation.

I could not continue with the charade after a few minutes, so I politely asked, "Who am I speaking with?"

She was silent for a while before she answered. It was obvious that she was disappointed that I could not recognize her voice. "How could you forget me? This is Fran. The only Francesca you knew from college."

My fingers tightened around the telephone receiver as if I was choking the last breath out of it. I looked at the thermostat on the wall, since my body was drenched in cold sweat. The temperature in my office was disappointingly normal, confirming what I already knew was happening to me; I was expressing a repressed anger of thirty-one years.

"Joseph, are you still there?"

I had to conceal what was happening to me when I answered her question. "I am very sorry, Francesca, but we have not spoken in thirty-one years." She was the last person I would expect to call me.

"Joseph, I am a CEO of a real estate holding company jointly owned by my husband and Wendy. You do remember Wendy from college? She resigned from the board of the corporation and requested that you take her place. Luckily, I found your office number from an internet search."

I was skeptical about what she was telling me. "Francesca, I last saw Wendy when we graduated from school thirty years ago. How could she appoint me to represent her interest? I am very sorry, but I have to decline the offer."

I heard a loud laughter coming from her. "You have not changed since our college days. Wendy signed over five percent of her interest in our corporation to you, because she felt that you taught us organizational skills and enviable work ethic in college, which probably contributed to our current success in life. The gesture from Wendy, and my approval, makes you one of the major shareholders of a multi-million dollar corporation. You need to talk to your accountant and lawyer about your legal obligations to the corporation. I am forwarding all the necessary paper work to you overnight." The receiver went dead after her last statement.

I was only eighteen years old when I met Francesca, and she was twenty-one. She had requested to be paired with me in a physics class project, and we became close friends. Studying together turned into a serious relationship in that small college town. Our relationship was convoluted and was mired in cross-cultural vicissitude. Our promising friendship faltered after she became a supermodel. What prejudice could not destroy was extinguished by fame and a lucrative modeling contract. I walked away from Francesca thirty-one years ago to save myself from self-indignation.

Fall of 1977

Chapter 2

I arrived at the small university town on a Saturday afternoon after traveling for more than 6,000 miles. I was excited when I left home but became homesick when I arrived at my dormitory. I spent a night in Chicago because I missed my connecting flight. The expansive international airport and bright city lights captivated my impressionable mind. The city was lit up by endless rows of street lights and lines of yellow taxis that waited for their turn to pick up passengers.

I arrived at the airport hotel lobby barely able to hear from a temporary auditory impairment caused by compression and decompression of the aircraft that brought me to Chicago. I enjoyed the benefits a four-star hotel offered courtesy of the airline that caused me to miss my connecting flight. A warm bubble bath, dimmed lights, and soft background music took me back to the last dinner I had at home with my family. No matter how hard I tried to suppress it, tears flowed profusely and blended with the soap suds all over me. I could not claim to have cried, because what I had was uncontrollable sobbing, like a child who missed his mother. Growing up had to wait.

The small university town airport was different from Chicago. There were no herds of passengers running to catch their next flight. Apart from the ten passengers who disembarked with me, the airport looked like an abandoned warehouse. No placard-carrying chauffeurs were in sight, and there were no signs that gave directions to the baggage claim area. I followed some of the passengers I felt knew where they were going to the baggage claim area. I collected my luggage and stepped outside the airport. It was a humid hot day that took away the last energy my body could muster after three days of limited sleep. There were no street lights found, and instead of lines of yellow taxis, there were two old station wagons waiting to pick up passengers.

The taxi driver I approached was polite but presented my first communication challenge. "Hi, need a cab?" His southern accent sounded like an unknown foreign language to me. It was after repeated enquiry from him that I realized what he was saying. I initially blamed my plugged ears, but it became obvious later that I could not understand southern colloquialism. However, we were able to effectively convey destination and cost to each other.

It took less than ten minutes to travel from the airport to my dormitory. The airport road was lined on both sides by pine trees. There was nothing remarkable or memorable about that short trip. I could not communicate with my driver, and the road deprived me of any remarkable scenery. It was a complete deprivation of verbal and visual stimulation.

I was apprehensive when the airport taxi dropped me off in front of my assigned residence hall. It was an old building with an overgrown lawn and a front door with a broken handle. It was not the type of building that was displayed on the cover of the college catalog. The ivy-covered administration building adorned the front cover of the school brochure, which was alluring. It was true that the academic standing of the university was the major reason why I chose to study there, but the majestic administration building probably lured me to the small college town. It was a place I wanted to call mine.

I was still sizing up the building when the taxi drove away. "This is my new home." I said under my breath. I lifted my suitcase and walked into a ramshackle lobby of the residence hall. I felt that it was a boys' residence hall that had seen better days. Chairs were strewn around, and a television set with a broken antenna sat on a sturdy desk.

The reception desk was manned by an elderly woman who was talking on the telephone. When she finally looked at me, she smiled and was apologetic. "I did not mean to ignore such a handsome man." She was probably in her late seventies and could be understood easily. I felt relieved that I could understand her diction.

"Thank you for the compliment. I am Joseph and a foreign student."

She looked at me again, adjusted her pair of eye glasses, and brought out a file box. "Does Joseph have a last name?" she asked.

I told her my last name, which made her chuckle. She searched through the file box and eventually came up with my folder. "This is for you, Joseph. It has your room key and signature card. Sign your card and give it back to me. Keep your key and the rest of the papers. You are assigned to Room 334. By the way, you have a funny last name."

She directed me to the side office, where I completed my dormitory registration. I was issued clean sheets and pillow cases. "Return your sheets weekly for clean ones," the desk clerk said. I thanked her and walked to the elevator. The sound of an old motor heralded the arrival of the elevator. When it stopped, its door squealed like a pig in distress while opening. I felt reluctant to walk into the elevator but had no other choice. The door took its time to close, and the trip to the third floor lasted longer than the time it took me to register at the reception desk. I listened to the churning of the mechanical pulley that sounded weaker as we approached the third floor. I disembarked without any mishap.

My dormitory room had a twin bed, a study desk, and a small closet. The room had no air conditioning, but it had a radiator next to the window. I inspected the radiator closely out of curiosity. Coming from a tropical country, I was not familiar with its function and wondered why such an ugly contraption was part of my room. I lifted the window shades and discovered that my room was overlooking a football practice field on the right and a football stadium on the left. It was a clear, sunny day, which made it easy for me to see newly constructed twin tower dormitories for females beyond the football stadium. The rest of the surrounding buildings were also newer than my dormitory. I felt that male freshmen were given the worst building on campus.

After I unpacked my suitcase and made my bed, I went back to the reception desk to ask for help. "Excuse me, how do I get to the dining room?"

It was not the same receptionist who had checked me in that attended to me when I returned for more help. The new receptionist was barely 20 years old and was probably a student. She opened a folder and brought out a piece of paper. She highlighted some areas before she handed over the piece of paper to me. "This is the campus map. We have only one central dining hall on campus. Breakfast, lunch, and dinner are served daily, except on Sundays. Only breakfast and dinner are served on Sundays. You may follow the highlighted area to the cafeteria."

I thanked her and left the building. I was able to find my way to the cafeteria. The dining hall had only a few students having lunch when I arrived. I walked to the food line and surveyed the food selection. I could not identify any of the available meal choices that could be seen through a protective glass. The lunch line was made up of new students who were too shy to speak to each other. The pervasive silence was intermittently broken when the food server asked for a student's choice. After a brief answer, the student returned to his or her state of self-imposed silence. I was too proud to ask for help in identifying the available choices of meal. I followed the silent group as if I knew what to stay when my turn came.

"What can I help you with?" the food server asked me.

I opened my mouth but could not speak. I was utterly embarrassed but refused to show my ignorance publically. I pointed to my choices without speaking.

"So, you want Swiss steak, mashed potato, and broccoli?"

I nodded my affirmation instead of saying yes. I took my tray to an empty table and sat down to eat. Most of the students were dining alone and were scattered all over the dining hall. Apart from the cacophony of sounds made by metallic utensils on dishes that were audible throughout the dining hall, there was no single conversation between the students. It was an eerie feeling, sitting there in total silence that afternoon, in a big cafeteria that could seat more than one thousand. It was not surprising that I became fixated on the annoying sounds that emanated from unintended multiple metallic utensils' encounters with dishes. Since that day, I have paid attention to how much noise I create when I eat.

# # #

I had difficulty sleeping on Sunday night, probably from jet lag. I lay on my hard mattress and relived some events from my childhood. Memorable events from my past rolled into my mind and watered my eyes with tears. At times, my face was graced with a needed smile. It was a melancholic state of being, brought about by loneliness. I was only 17 years old, thousands of miles away from home, and a first-year college student. I had to quickly disabuse myself of the false notion that self-pity or negative introspection is good for personal growth.

"You are going far away from home by your choice. You have to grow up faster than you may want. We will always be here for you." Those were my father's words before I left home. As my father's words haunted me that night, I got out of bed, walked to my desk, and turned my light on. I opened my Catholic version of the Holy Bible to Psalm 131:1-2 and read out loud.

"*Lord, I have given up my pride,*

  and turned away from my arrogance.

I am not concerned with great matters,

  or with subjects too difficult for me.

Instead, I am content and at peace.

As a child lies quietly in its mother's arms,

  so my heart is quiet within me."

I closed my Bible, crawled back into bed, and fell asleep.

# # #

Monday morning finally arrived. I woke up very early and felt rested. I was probably the only one awake that early in the morning in my dormitory. It gave me the opportunity for a private bathroom time. Each bathroom was shared by eight students. We had enough stalls for all the students but there was no privacy. It became my routine to wake up early every day throughout my stay in the freshman dormitory.

I brushed my teeth longer than is normal for me, since I had time. When I walked into the shower stall, I opted for a very warm shower, which I found very soothing. I could not help but sing as the warm water cascaded from my head, through my body, and finally to the fenestrated draining hole on the floor. The shower started as a trickle and then flooded my body as I increased the volume of water flow. I felt rejuvenated when it was over. I quickly dried my body and went back to my room to choose what to wear for my first official school day. I settled on a pair of blue pants and a white shirt. I had no casual clothes and had to wear dress pants. I must have looked odd to the rest of the students, since most wore blue jeans.

Class registration started at eight in the morning. My registration was complicated because I had to obtain clearance papers from the international students' office before I could be assigned to my chosen classes. All the immigration papers issued to me by the US embassy had to be presented to the international students' adviser.

It was a long walk from my dormitory to the international students' office. The warm humid August weather made the heat unbearable. Leaves on most of the trees stood still, since no measurable wind was blowing. Without any wind, sweat came out of my pores and stuck like glue. The campus plan given to me on arrival was helpful. I had spent Sunday afternoon identifying all the major buildings in school. It was therefore easy for me that Monday morning to locate the school administration building. I hurried to get to my destination, but my increased energy utilization made my sweating worse. Students darted from one building to another as they registered and presented their registration cards to various academic departments.

I was sweating profusely when I arrived at the administration building. I was very self-conscious and felt the need to dry my face in the bathroom before walking into the adviser's office. The building was air conditioned and therefore provided a quick cooling effect on my body. When I looked in the mirror, I discovered some wet spots on my shirt. It was not a flattering sight, and it had to be remedied. I fanned my shirt with a magazine I found lying around. When I felt that some of the wet areas on my shirt had faded away, I left the bathroom for my unofficial appointment. I felt that my action was not out of vanity but rather from my belief that first impression mattered a lot. I did not want to walk into an office sweating and be judged wrongly on my first day in school.

I walked into the international students' office very confident and with a beaming smile. I barely looked around before I sat down on one of the available chairs in the waiting room. I inspected my documents several times before I paid attention to my surroundings. The waiting area had ten chairs, side tables with old lamps, and international magazines. At one end of the room was a secretarial desk that was unmanned when I arrived. The room had no windows and was poorly lit. Hanging on the walls were photographs of some world-renowned politicians with their year of graduation from the school emblazoned in brass. I was mesmerized with the notable graduates and their various accomplishments. For a fleeting second, I imagined my own photograph hanging on the wall. I smiled as I erased such grandiose thinking from my mind. I reasoned that only world-renowned politicians were given such recognition, and not scientists. It was therefore clear to me, as a future scientist, that I would not be accorded such recognition in the future.

"What time is it?" a sweet female voice asked me.

I looked around and was surprised that someone spoke to me. Sitting in front of me were two female students. They wore faded blue jean pants and cotton tops. One of the girls smiled when our eyes met. Her face had no blemishes, and her dimples accentuated her beauty. She had beautiful, long, golden hair that flowed to the middle of her back. Her skin was as smooth as dry alabaster, which glowed as she shifted from her chair. She adjusted her sleeves as she became aware of my visual scrutiny. I could not look away as she continued to smile. Her eye brows were perfectly done and symmetrical. Her lips quivered as she spoke to me.

"Hello, I am Wendy and a sophomore."

I was totally disarmed by her beauty. I mumbled my name, as if I was not sure. "I am Joseph and a foreigner." I felt like a bumbling fool with such an introduction.

"Welcome to our school, Joseph. Are you a freshman?"

I was about to answer her question when she introduced her friend to me.

"Joseph, this is my friend Lisa." Lisa smiled but did not speak.

I stood up, walked over to Wendy, and shook her hand.

"Joseph, how long have you been in my country?" Wendy said.

It was obvious that Wendy wanted to know more about me. "I am a new student. I have been here for only two days." But I was asked into the conference room before I could fully answer Wendy's question. When I stood up to go into the conference room, Wendy stood up too and shook my hand again. I could not hide my uneasiness as sweat poured down from my face. It was obvious that I lost my composure, probably from shyness.

I barely paid attention to my foreign student adviser. My only interest was to go back to the waiting room to finish my conversation with Wendy. The only thing I heard clearly was when Mr. Green stood up to see me out and said, "Joseph, do you have any questions?"

I shook his hand and said, "No, thank you." He handed me the signed forms for my registration and wished me a successful school year. I rushed out to the waiting room, but Wendy and Lisa were gone. I was partly relieved because I did not know what I would have said to them. It was an annoying feeling of ambivalence that took over me as I walked out of the office. As I stepped out of the building, I looked in all directions, searching for Wendy, and could not find her. I was in a hurry and could not go back to the office to search for them. I walked away disappointed.

I registered for seven classes instead of the traditional five classes. I had two goals at that time; keep busy, and graduate in three years. I stopped by the bookstore before going back to my residence hall and bought all the books I needed for my classes. I took my new books to my room before going to the cafeteria for lunch.

Chapter 3

I could not find solace in my room. The temperature had soared by noon, and my room was hot. I opened my windows to let in air, but what I felt was hot and suffocating. I opened my door to create a wind drift effect that might help cool my room. As I sat on my desk close to the window and pondered on what to do next, my next door neighbors stopped by to introduce themselves. My open door had served as an invitation for them to venture in.

"Hello, I am Cecil, and here is Jake." They were taller than most of the students I had met so far.

"I am Joseph and a freshman." Before I could finish introducing myself, Cecil's curiosity got the best of him.

"Where are you from, man? You have an accent."

I told Cecil the same story I had told so many students and administrators since I'd arrived at the school. I could tell that he lost interest after less than one minute of my narration because he probably wanted a shortened version of my life story. I felt that I failed to answer his question in a succinct way without embellishment. All he wanted to know was my country of origin, which I could have answered with a one-word answer. It was lost on me that they were male freshmen students with short attention spans. It was therefore not surprising that they showed no interest in my boring story of preoccupation with adventure.

When they were bored enough with my narcissistic tale, they scampered for my open door with a lame excuse. "Catch you later, man," was their polite way of telling me that they'd had enough of my story. My interaction with Cecil and Jake taught me a valuable lesson about the attention span of young male college students. I had to quickly analyze in the future the version of my life story my audience might prefer. It became one of the early adaptations I made in my communication skills. It appeared that my education began before I even set foot in the classroom.

After my experience with Cecil, I reanalyzed my interaction with Wendy earlier in the day. She had asked simple questions that required one-word answers, but I'd turned it into flirtatious verbal gymnastics. It was not obvious to me when it was going on, because I'd been bemused by her beauty and may have been inadvertently hypnotized by the flattering dimples that punctuated her cheeks. I had seen beautiful women before, but nothing like Wendy, who was the embodiment of natural elegance.

There I was, hot, sweating from the choking heat in my room, and the only thing I worried about was my interaction with a stranger I'd met that morning. I had many other reasons for my preoccupation with Wendy; she was erudite, elegant, personable, and could be classified as an egalitarian. My preoccupation, therefore, was not a lustful reverie, but rather a captivation by amiable natural qualities.

Chapter 4

Classes started after a few days of freshman orientation. It was a time for freshmen to get acquainted with the school, and with each other. Social activities that were supposed to make us enjoy our new found freedom and temporarily forget our family failed to achieve either goal for me. I attended a few of the events out of boredom and was ready for classes to start. For lack of anything else to do, I read some introductory chapters from my textbooks. Reading science textbooks shifted my mind from fantasy to critical thinking. There was no further invasion of my rational thoughts by unrealistic wasteful daydreaming when I delved into scientific concepts that needed my undivided attention.

Some aspects of college freshman orientation were beneficial, but most of the time spent in the various activities was wasted. All the orientation necessary could have been done in a day. To the school's credit, we were taught how to survive and succeed in college. For foreign male students, we had a special program on cultural differences and how to avoid awkward social situations. The emphasis was on the subtleties of verbal communication with our peers and how to respect our female counterparts. It was a significant reminder to me that it was not what I said that mattered a lot of times, but more importantly, how I said it. Words were powerful weapons that had to be used cautiously, since they can maim like real weapons do. Well-crafted words could also be used to negotiate a peaceful surrender, even with the most hardened soul. I also appreciated more the fact that I communicated, even before I spoke. A smile or a frown, even before I spoke, defined the content and limits of my communication. My analysis of the encounters I'd had since I came to school reverted to my encounter with Wendy. I flattered myself by blaming our flirtation on my engaging eye contact.

# # #

Although I'd read several chapters on molecular biology, I was apprehensive when I arrived at the lecture hall. It was a big classroom that could seat up to 200 students. The chairs were arranged in a semicircle, with higher elevations in the back rows. Wherever you sat, the professor was always visible, even if you were short. Spotlighting was focused on the lecture lectern, while the rest of the room was dimly lit.

The professor was sitting down and looking over her notes when I walked in. She was immersed in her reading and appeared oblivious to all the noise students were making inside the lecture hall. I walked over to her desk and presented my registration card. I sat down on one of the first row seats and opened my textbook. It was not long after I sat down that an enticing floral scent tickled my nasal passages, and a sweet voice whispered in my left ear.

"Hello Joseph."

The voice was familiar and was more enticing than the first time I heard it. She was so close when she spoke that her warm, fresh breath caressed my neck and sent unintended shudders down my spine. I was visibly startled, to her delight.

"Are you afraid of me?" she asked.

"I am not afraid of you, Wendy. I did not expect to see you in my class. I was just surprised, that is all."

As I turned to look at her again, she taunted me with an alluring smile and a whispered reproach. I fixed my gaze at her smile as my hands trembled, and my lips quivered. When my tongue became untied, I spoke with self-assurance. "Wendy, I am happy to see you in my class," I finally said.

She continued with her quips as I tried hard to gain control of the situation. "I did not know that you owned the class, Joseph."

I accorded her the honor of having the last say, but I never accepted a defeat. The professor inadvertently ended the verbal jousting as soon as she began to introduce herself. Once the lecture started, I lost interest in Wendy. I was immersed on the new concept of molecular and cellular biology. It was the mid 1970s, and the lecture was perceived as a novel concept. It was fascinating to be lectured by one of the pioneers in the field. I was impressed with her lecture style and her depth of knowledge. She was one of the first authors of a comprehensive textbook in cellular and molecular biology. I felt privileged to be in her class as a freshman. I was allowed to take her class because of my strong science background in high school.

I could not sit still in my chair as the lecture progressed. I shifted from side to side to have a better view of some of her illustrations, and raised my hand twice to ask questions. Her answers were very informative, and she thanked me for my thought-provoking questions.

Wendy turned toward me at the end of the lecture with a puzzled look on her face. "Joseph, are you always this attentive in class?" I looked at her and smiled. "Are you one of those geniuses?" she asked. "You did not take any notes during the lecture," she continued.

I was compelled to answer her question. "Taking notes during lectures divides your attention between the lecture and what you are writing." She nodded her head in agreement. "I also read the required chapters before coming to class today, which made it easier for me to understand most of the new concept she introduced to us. My belief is that every word from the professor is very important, therefore, writing every word down is almost impossible. Understanding the concept is more important than writing everything down."

After I finished what I had to say, she realized that she could not win the argument. She looked at me, and in a low tone she said, "Joseph, you are a handful."

I had barely two minutes left before my next class in the adjoining building when I looked at my watch. As I excused myself, Wendy extended her hand to me while still sitting down. I shook her hand and held on to it for a while. "You are going to be late to your next class Joseph." I released her hand and walked toward the exit door. She stood up and followed me.

As I walked out of the classroom, Wendy asked, "Joseph, do you have lunch plans?" I was not sure what she meant by lunch plans. "We could meet for lunch in the school cafeteria if you had no other plans for the afternoon," she said.

I felt privileged to be asked to have lunch with Wendy, so I accepted the offer without further consideration. We agreed to meet at the entrance of the cafeteria at noon. Yet I sensed that she felt uneasy after she asked me to have lunch with her. I was in a hurry to get to my class, so I did not worry about her state of mind. However, I was excited that a beautiful sophomore student asked me to have lunch with her.

# # #

Wendy was standing in front of the cafeteria when I finally arrived for lunch. There were two other students with her. From a distance, they looked like runway models waiting for their turn to strut for their captivated audience. I was not their only audience, since passing students turned around to take second looks at the three beautiful women waiting for a freshman foreign student.

As I got closer, Wendy beamed with a smile and was outwardly excited to see me. "Joseph, meet Francesca and Debbie, my sorority sisters." Francesca barely looked at me, but Debbie shook my hand. Francesca was very tall and beautiful. However, she was not friendly. She was very different from Wendy. While she enhanced her beauty with facial makeup, Wendy was a natural beauty without any artificial help.

Francesca wore a flowing pink summer dress and open-toe pumps. Her high heels asserted themselves in a noisy cafeteria with their own rhythmic sounds as she walked to the food line. Her walk was a gleeful prance with constant flipping of long curly hair away from her face. She delightfully flaunted her beauty as young men turned around several times to have better glimpse of her.

Wendy was very reserved and was not the type who would call undue attention to herself. She was very beautiful but did not celebrate her natural beauty. She preferred to engage in scholarly discussions, instead of wasting energy on superficial nihilistic pseudo tantrums exhibited by some college coeds.

Debbie was just an enabler who fed Francesca's ego with constant compliments. She did not contribute much to any of our discussions. She was very beautiful but appeared insecure.

We spent more than forty-five minutes in the cafeteria listening to Francesca's summer vacation stories. She bragged about her summer modeling jobs with department stores. She was paid well, according to her, and she was also given free clothing from choice women stores. She was delighted with the proceeds from her quasi modeling career and was looking forward to future engagements.

"Wendy, tell me, why does a beautiful girl like you refuse to model?" Francesca said.

Wendy fell into her trap by answering her question. "I am not as beautiful as you, Francesca."

Wendy's answer brought about further discussion on the qualities that made Francesca special. I felt nauseated as Francesca beamed with her fake smile. I was disgusted with Francesca's self- adulation and decided to end my failed lunch date with Wendy. I had expected a private lunch with my new friend but instead, I had been exposed to the most conceited girl on campus. I had to wait for another opportunity to get to know Wendy better.

When Francesca stood up to leave after lunch, she announced to her sorority sisters that a new modeling agency had offered her a contract. She ignored me as she walked away. Wendy apologized to me for her friend's indifference. "Francesca can be overbearing sometimes, but she means no harm."

Debbie defended her friend before Wendy could finish what she was telling me.

"I prefer a girl with good moral character rather than a beauty queen," I said after Francesca had left. They laughed at my statement. My feelings were hurt by Francesca's superciliousness, and they knew it.

"See you around, Joseph," Wendy said before she walked away. I stood by the entrance of the cafeteria and watched her walk to her residence hall without looking back.

Chapter 5

I developed a fulfilling friendship with Wendy that was emotionally rewarding and intellectually stimulating over a short period of time. She had travelled extensively in Europe with her parents and was knowledgeable in so many areas. She could discuss science, art, music, and world politics very comfortably. Her father was an executive of a multinational corporation, and her mother was a university professor. They vacationed in the south of France every summer, where she learned the French language. She took me to several museums in nearby cities to supplement my general college education requirements and helped me in conversational French.

"Joseph, it is very important to see and feel what you learn in school. It makes it easier to retain the material you learn if you can relate your learning to practical experiences you've had," Wendy said to me.

We were regular visitors at art shows and botanical gardens. She wowed me with her knowledge of plant species. Weekends I spent with Wendy were like guided tours to foreign countries. We once visited an art museum where a landscape painting from the south of France captivated Wendy. As she viewed the art piece, her face glowed, and her fingers trembled. With outward pride, she went into vivid descriptions of that area of France, so that when I closed my eyes, I felt as if I was there walking with Wendy to the local bistro. When I opened my eyes, she was looking at me intently with her red chapeau tilted upward to reveal her piercing green eyes.

"I am very sorry for acting distracted. I was daydreaming about your place in the south of France, Wendy."

She smiled without showing her perfect teeth. "You can spend the summer with us next year in France, if you are interested. I am sure my parents would love to have you. We could have so much fun together, Joseph."

It was obvious that she was sincere with her offer, but I felt that we did not know each other that well to be planning a summer vacation together. "Thank you for the offer Wendy, but I have plans to go to summer school." As we passed a group of high school students she stopped to talk to their teacher.

# # #

I studied with Wendy, Lisa, and Debbie every week night from the time school started. We rarely talked about social events during study periods. However, Wendy broke with our tradition one Thursday night. "Joseph I would like to talk to you privately for a few minutes."

We walked out to a moonlit humid night and sat on the steps at the entrance to the library. I was very anxious to find out what was so important to Wendy that she needed a private discussion with me. Her face wore a disarming smile that was accentuated by the bright moonlight. Her demeanor made it difficult to tell the seriousness of her summons. I waited until she was ready to talk. "My parents are coming to visit me next week during my sorority talent show. I would like to introduce you to them. Daddy wants to meet this Joseph I talk about all the time."

I was relieved that it was a simple request. I was afraid that I might have unknowingly offended her. "It would be a privilege to meet your parents," I said.

"Thank you so much, Joseph. I will get a ticket for you to attend the talent show." She placed her hand on my shoulder and gave me a friendly squeeze. We left the bright night behind and walked into the library. Debbie and Linda were curious about our sudden departure, but they did not ask where we had gone. Their mischievous smile betrayed their inner thoughts. We let them wallow in their fantasies as we looked at each other and laughed haughtily.

"Did you guys go out to make out?"

Debbie's question took me by surprise. I felt compelled to tell them what had transpired outside. "We were outside discussing your sorority talent show," I said. Although they did not believe what I said, Wendy made no effort to correct their error in judging us. They were left with the false impression that we had a secret love affair.

# # #

Wendy's sorority talent show was held at the student center on a Friday night. The hall was turned into a formal ballroom with red and white draperies hung on the tall windows. Red and white sorority banners also adorned the walls, while helium filled floating balloons were held back by tall ceilings. Sorority members wore red dresses, white scarfs, and red hats. They meandered and exchanged witty repartee in the hallway. Their somber male courtiers wore white tuxedo and white bowties. It was a program for women, and the few men that attended were not as elated as their female counterparts.

I tried to look my best for Wendy, since I was her guest. I wore a pencil striped navy blue suit and a white shirt because I was not a courtier. Wendy was waiting at the door when I walked in with red roses for her. She looked more beautiful than I had ever seen her. Her long golden hair was in a French braid and was partially covered by her red hat.

"Thank you, Joseph, for the red roses. You make me feel special."

I had a brief moment when my level of happiness reached a state of inexplicable euphoria. I closed my eyes to savor that special moment, but I quickly realized that it was not an appropriate time for reverie. When I opened my eyes, she was still standing in front of me. As my lips quivered, I blurted out what I saw. "You look beautiful, Wendy." I paused briefly and then continued to express my gratitude to her. "Thank you for inviting me to your talent show."

She hugged me, took the roses from me, and held onto my arm. She walked graciously over to her parents while still holding onto my arm.

Her father was taller than six foot and athletically built. He wore a white tuxedo, since he was his wife's courtier. "Dad, this is Joseph," Wendy said to her father.

He shook my hand more firmly than I anticipated and caused slight pain to my fingers. When he let go of my hand, the pain, however, lingered on. "So, you are Joseph?" His question was rhetorical, so I did not answer it.

Her mother waited patiently to be introduced. She was gracious and looked younger than her age of forty-five. "You look more like a twin sister to Wendy than her mother," I said to her. My comment was an honest observation and not a cheap flattery.

"It is nice to finally meet you, Joseph. Wendy has told us so much about you," she said. When the introductions were done, they asked me to sit with them. We walked to their assigned table, stopping occasionally to say hello to their friends. I was about to sit down when the master of ceremonies asked for the opening prayer. The noise in the hall died instantly as the prayer commenced.

Wendy thrilled the audience with her piano recital. Her fingers caressed the keyboard as if she was practicing a sensual massage. I watched her performance very attentively but was aware that her father was distracted by my presence. He looked at me from head to toe several times and probably wondered what his daughter found appealing in me. When our eyes met during intermission, he used the opportunity to speak to me. "I was told that you are a good student. We are happy that you are Wendy's study partner."

I was surprised that he gave me a compliment. I had expected a warning from him about his daughter. "Thank you," was the only thing I said. My legs shook uncontrollably under the table out of fear. It was my first experience with a protective father of a beautiful girl.

Her mother sensed my uneasiness and joined the conversation, probably to alleviate my anxiety. "Joseph, you need to visit us soon. Try to come with Wendy next time she visits home." Her mother's invitation reassured me that she had no ill feelings toward me.

"Thank you for the invitation. I will try my best to visit soon." I said to her.

In the presence of Wendy's parents, I felt inadequate. I could not imagine why a rich beautiful girl was wasting her time with me. "I guess my wit and handsomeness are good enough for Wendy," I murmured under my breath. I smiled at my silliness. Fortunately, no one heard what I said.

Occasionally, Wendy's mother looked at me and smiled. I was aware that they watched everything I did. I declined the meal I was served to avoid further scrutiny. "Joseph, what type of food do you eat?" Wendy's mother asked me. She probably wondered why I turned down my meal.

"I am not hungry, that is all. I eat everything, except fish and pork," I answered her question very politely. She appeared to be satisfied with my answer and continued with her meal.

I left the talent show a few minutes before it ended. However, I apologized to Wendy's parents for leaving early. "I have a project due on Monday and I need to wake up early in the morning to finish it. Let Wendy know that I had fun tonight and why I left early." When I was done reciting my excuse, they shook my hand before I left the hall.

"Have a good night, Joseph," they said in unison.

I was not able to say goodbye to Wendy because she was sitting with her sorority sisters. I sauntered out of the hall into the warm breezy night and wondered what Wendy's parents thought about me. Since I was not in a hurry, I took a longer path back to my hot desolate room and unforgiving hard dormitory mattress. I was not aware that I was sweating until I reached my dormitory, because my senses had been numbed by unrealistic introspection.

# # #

I woke up on Saturday morning to the sound of the intercom in my room. Our receptionist's voice followed the buzzing sound. "Joseph, a guest is waiting for you in the lobby."

I wondered who could be looking for me that early on a Saturday morning. It was my first visitor since I'd moved into the dormitory. I did not want to receive a guest without my morning shower, so I had to prevaricate for time. "Please ask my guest to give me a few minutes to dress up," I said to the receptionist. I got dressed after I took a quick shower. Since I was not sure who was looking for me, I got dressed for the day.

I was surprised to see Wendy standing by the entrance door of my dormitory. She wore a fitted pair of blue jeans, a red cotton shirt, and a pair of sandals that exposed her red painted toenails. She ran to hug me as if we were lovers separated for a long time. We held on to each other for a long time as if we knew that premature physical separation would take us back to reality. What we had was a friendship that was occasionally lured to the boundary of a love affair.

It was hard to tell how long we held each other, but holding on longer could not solve our predicament. It was apparent that we were attracted to each other but were afraid to mess up a good friendship with premature romance. When reality tempered our initial exuberance, Wendy remembered what she wanted to tell me. "Thank you for last night, Joseph. I love my roses." The expression of her gratitude included a kiss on the cheek. "Why did you leave last night without saying goodbye?" she asked me.

"I was very tired and needed to go to sleep early. I am very sorry for being inconsiderate." I lied to Wendy.

It was apparent that she did not believe my excuse. "Did my Daddy upset you? He can be very protective of me sometimes. He is aware that we are just friends, but I am not sure he believed me," Wendy said to me. After several minutes of probing my inner thoughts, she finally told me why she came to visit me. "I have a big surprise for you, Joseph. Are you willing to travel with me?"

I smiled as if I knew where we were going. "Do you expect me to turn down an offer from you, Wendy? I am not sure where we are going, but I am sure that I will have fun with you."

She ran toward the exit door as if hoping that I would run after her. We acted like grade school children chasing after each other. As she stopped to wait for me, I passed her and held the door for her. She grabbed my waist to pull me away from the door. It was a flirtatious frolicking that challenged the boundaries of our mere friendship. "I am very happy that you are going home with me today. My mother invited us for breakfast. We have to hurry to get there on time."

Cold sweat poured down my face as I looked at Wendy with bewilderment. "We are having breakfast with your family?"

She hesitated before she said, "My mother and Scott are the only ones at home. My father left for Europe earlier this morning for a meeting. My mother had no other plans, so she wanted us to spend the day with her."

I followed Wendy to her red convertible Italian sports car. Even in the early morning sunshine, it stood out with its bright red color and polished wheels. There was no doubt that it belonged to her. She had a red scarf tied to the stem of the rear mirror. "Wendy I am confused," I said to her. She looked at me as if she was waiting for me to finish what I was saying. "I am not sure what I like more; you or your car."

She threw her car key at me. "Joseph, so my car is more important to you than our friendship?"

I placed the fingers of my right hand on my head as if I was thinking about what was more important to me. "After serious consideration, I have decided that you are more important to me than a red fancy car." I gave her keys back to her.

She retrieved her pair of sunshades and a hair band from her purse before she started the car. She leaned over and adjusted my seat before she drove away. Several students watched in awe as her engine roared with each change of gear. She turned into a major road and took off as if she was in a hurry. Her hair band was very effective in holding her hair in place as wind challenged us with every increase in the car speed. "Brace yourself, Joseph. We are off to my hometown. Don't let stupid wind whip you into submission, since we are driving top down all the way."

I looked at her and asked, "Where is my friend Wendy? You don't act or sound like her anymore."

She smiled. "This is my alter ego, Joe."

I was puzzled by what she called me. "Joe? No one's ever called me Joe."

She laughed sadistically, changed her gear, and sped away.

# # #

It was difficult to hold any meaningful conversation with Wendy as we travelled through windy country roads.

Most of our conversations were small talk. In search of something to hold my interest as we passed several cultivated and expansive farms, I watched tobacco leaves swayed by the wind we created as we sped through the narrow roads.

She knew that I was bored with farms and felt the need to start a conversation to keep my mind occupied. "My parents moved to this area 20 years ago. I was too young to remember details of our move. Although I love the area, I plan to move away after I finish school."

I turned to her with a puzzled look. "Wendy, farms are not for me. I am a city boy. I grew up in a densely populated commercial coastal town. The night lights and noisy streets captivated me. I will take you there some day."

She was elated by my offer. "Are you serious, Joseph? Can we go to your hometown next summer after we travel to the south of France?"

If I answered yes, it meant that I'd accepted the invitation to France. "I told you that I will be going to summer school. However, let's see how next summer turns out," was the only appropriate answer I could give her.

# # #

It took close to 30 minutes of her careful driving through winding country roads to reach her city. It was a tranquil drive except for the roaring noise from Wendy's car muffler. Although we passed several small towns, her city was bigger than our college town. When we finally

reached her house, I reluctantly got out of the car. No colorful description could do justice to the opulent mansion that stood before me. The imposing mahogany doors complemented the quarry stone walls. There was an abundance of trees that provided needed shades throughout their ten-acre property.

"Wow! I love your house." My comment probably influenced her decision to show their swimming pool and two tennis courts first. When we were done touring the outside facilities, we entered her house through the back door, which led into her father's gun collection room. Polished mahogany paneled walls with built-in gun shelves gave the area a distinctive look.

"Most of the guns were collected by my grandfather, but my father added some collections from the 1700s," Wendy told me. It was obvious that Wendy was proud of her heritage and was eager to impress me with her knowledge of history. Each gun display had an inscription with a detailed history of the gun. We were still in the gun room when Wendy's mother and brother joined us. "Mom, you do remember Joseph?" Wendy jokingly said.

Her mother shook my hand. "Welcome to our home, Joseph. This is my son, Scott."

Scott shook my hand too and said, "Nice to meet you, Joseph."

It took close to 30 minutes to complete the tour of her house. I was given an extensive lecture on antique furniture, which they had abundance of. Their wine cellar was the last place we visited. It was her mother's favorite place. Wendy's mother schooled me on the importance of temperature control in a wine cellar and the detrimental effect of excessive heat to aging red wine. "Joseph, fine wines have to be pampered. The temperature and humidity have to be maintained at acceptable levels all the time," she said.

The woodwork in the cellar was a masterpiece. Bottles of wine were arranged by country of origin and year of grape. I pretended to be interested, since it apparently meant a lot to her. "Thank you for inviting me to your beautiful house. How do you find time to take care of such a big place?"

I was in mid-sentence when she pointed to the schedule on the wall. "I have a house keeper who comes to help me three times a week. She is the person who keeps the place tidy." As we concluded the tour of the wine cellar, she closed the cellar door and reset the temperature.

We walked to the breakfast room, where we finally sat down. I sat next to Wendy by her mother's request. She sat across from us and watched our interaction attentively. Breakfast was an assortment of local favorites; omelets, pancakes, sausages, bacon, fruits, and juices. Tea and coffee were available but were not served, since none of us wanted a warm beverage.

"Joseph, tell me a little more about your family. Do you have brothers and sisters?"

I talked about my parents and all my siblings.

She was fascinated by my courage to leave home at a tender age to carve out my own identity. "You are so courageous, Joseph. I am sure that Wendy will learn a lot from you."

We proceeded to their drawing room after breakfast. Her mother led the way. I followed Wendy, while Scott left us without announcing his departure. After we were seated, Wendy's mother continued to ask me pointed questions. "What is your long-term plan, Joseph?"

I was confused by the question and needed clarification. "I am very sorry, but I am not sure what you meant by my long-term plan."

She laughed. "I was just curious about your professional goal."

I was just a freshman in college and had nothing profound to tell her. "I love sciences and have not made up my mind yet about a career." I knew what I would like to do professionally but was uncomfortable discussing it with her. Sensing that I was uncomfortable with her barrage of questions, she excused herself to make a telephone call. I could not tell if I passed the various tests I was subjected to that morning. I found solace in the fact that I tried to be myself and nothing more.

After ten minutes of waiting for her mother, Wendy invited me to her room to listen to music. Her bedroom was very large with a separate sitting area. It was elaborately decorated with paintings and tasseled draperies. She had a queen-sized bed, a desk, and a loveseat. It was odd that her sorority colors were not adequately represented in her bedroom. She had a collection of teddy bears and stuffed elephants. Her classical music album collections were arranged neatly by their composers. Her poster as a ballerina featured prominently at the head of her bed.

"I wish I'd known you when you were a ballerina. I would have loved to see you dance," I said to Wendy while admiring her poster.

She opened a trunk and brought out a photo album. "Do you like classical music, Joseph?" She was walking to the area where her music albums were displayed when she asked the question. "My father played classical music on our gramophone when I was very young. I was not interested in classical music at that time." She picked out one of the albums and placed it on the turntable. "Joseph, I am about to play Dvorak's *New World Symphony* for you. It is my favorite symphony." She talked about the importance of the symphony to American classical music history. As the sound of music filled her bedroom, she closed her eyes and bopped her head in a rhythmic fashion. For a moment I lost her to a music-induced state of ecstasy. She hurriedly stopped the music and changed the album to a classical dance composition. She took her shoes off, then stretched her arms and legs. When the music started, she twirled and spun around as if she was suspended by a fulcrum. She was standing on the tips of her toes, which at times looked like they were suspended in the air. I watched in disbelief as I was privately entertained by an acclaimed dancer. As the tempo of the music increased, she became more daring with her acrobatics.

I heard clapping from the hallway where her mother probably stood and watched her daughter perform for me. "Bravo! Bravo! Bravo! Joseph must be very special for you to dance for him with such an effort," her mother said.

Wendy stopped dancing when she heard her mother. "I am very sorry, mom, I got carried away." Her mother walked into her room and hugged her.

"Wendy, you are very good. Why did you stop dancing?" I said to her.

She walked closer to me before she answered my question. "I have not danced in a long time, Joseph. I injured my ankle four years ago and gave up dancing after that." Her mother opened one of the closets to show me all the prizes Wendy won from dancing.

"Mom we have to get back to school before the football game. I promised my friends that I would go to the game with them."

Her mother looked at her and said, "I wish you could stay longer. I miss not having you around."

Wendy had to come up with a different reason to leave. "I am sure Joseph is tired of hanging around with me all morning. He probably wants to get back to school."

I could not disagree with Wendy, so I kept quiet. "I hope you come back to see us again, Joseph." Her open invitation sounded sincere.

"I am very grateful for your hospitality." I said to her. We shook hands before I walked out. Scott was standing by Wendy's car to say goodbye to us.

Wendy barely spoke after we got in the car. I was concerned that I probably let her down in front of her mother. She finally said, "I miss home."

I was relieved by her confession of missing home. "I miss my family, too," I said to her. The rest of our drive was uneventful.

We were close to my dormitory when Wendy asked what I thought of her family. "Your family is very rich, and you have a marvelous house."

She slapped my knee gently and said, "That is not what I asked you, Joe."

I told her that it was an honor to be invited to her house. "Your mother is very nice and appears to be very caring." She did not respond to my comment, so I continued. "Wendy, why do you need my friendship?"

Her answer was not elaborate. "Joseph, you are a good student, a hard worker, and a good soul."

I was not sure what she meant by a good soul. It was probably a colorful way of telling me that she liked me. She made another request before she left me. "Joseph, do you mind taking me to the football game tonight?"

It was a surprise request that I could not say no to. "I will be honored to spend the rest of the day with you, my ballerina."

She smiled and said, "You are such a tease, Joseph."

I chuckled, since Wendy was wrong with her assessment of me. I disembarked from her car and waved goodbye.

Before she drove away, she yelled out to me, "By the way, Joseph, come to my dorm an hour before the game so that we can have more time to talk."

#

It was my first football game. The football field was crowded and noisy. We found our seats and joined the festive crowd. It was the first home game of the year. When the cheerleaders came out to wow the audience with their acrobatics, Francesca was the leading majorette. She twirled her baton as high as she could and, without looking up, held out her hand to catch it.

"Way to go, Francesca," Wendy shouted as loud as possible. It was not an event for meaningful conversation because of the loud noise. We clapped, yelled, and screamed for the duration of the game. Our team scored first, which caused our school band to go into a frenzy with loud drumming and booming French horns. The rest of us joined in singing the school's favorite game song. Our noisy rendition boomed and reverberated across the stadium, silencing the referee's whistle. We had similar celebrations after every touchdown our team made. We won the game to the delight of all the students who attended. We celebrated our win very colorfully.

When the football game was over, I followed Wendy to where the cheerleaders were congregated. Francesca was eagerly waiting for her friends to give their biased opinion of her performance. "Francesca, you were great. You are very acrobatic," I said to her.

Francesca shook my hand for the first. "Thank you, honey," Francesca said to me, in her exaggerated southern drawl.

As they carried on with hugs and loud noise, I excused myself. Wendy followed me to the section gate of the field. "Thank you, Joseph, for making my day special," she said me. I smiled bashfully and thanked her for making my weekend exciting. She hurriedly hugged me and walked away without giving me an opportunity for a rejoinder. It was an anticlimactic end to a riveting unofficial first date.

I was not sure how to show Wendy my appreciation for the wonderful day I had with her. Most of the things I thought about doing for her would have depleted my limited financial resources. She was aware of my minor financial predicament, because I'd asked for her advice recently when I ran out of school meal cards. Instead of advising me on how to conserve my limited resources, she gave me all her meal cards, since she rarely ate at the school cafeteria. She had a favorite bistro where she bought her dinner and occasionally ordered pizza. I thought about asking her out to a movie, but I had to find out how much it would cost me. As I pondered over my choices, my father's words kept haunting me. "You have to live within your means when you get to college, my son." I shelved the idea of going to the movies with Wendy. Instead, I wrote thank you notes to Wendy and her mother.

Chapter 6

I worked very hard in school and was considered an outstanding student by several science departments. My obsession with learning became worse as the semester progressed. Occasionally on weekends, I forgot to leave the library before the cafeteria closed and had to settle for what vending machines had to offer. I excelled in all my classes but wanted to be the best student in every class I took. It would have been unpardonable for me to travel thousands of miles to go to school and wind up being an academic slouch.

Many professors asked me to consider working for them during the summer as a research assistant. It was an honor rarely bestowed on a first semester freshman student. A few days before Thanksgiving break, I had a meeting with the chairman of my department by his request. I arrived at my meeting not knowing what the meeting was about. I was doing well in all my classes and was not concerned. Professor Ezir, the chairman of my department, was in his early 70s. He was slightly over-weight and a chain pipe smoker. His stained white labo-ratory coat set him apart from the rest of the chemistry faculty. It was known that he worked diligently in his research laboratory and published more research papers yearly than the rest of chemistry faculty put together. He barely had time to fuss about his dirty white coat.

"Good morning. I am Joseph. I have an appointment with Professor Ezir," I said to his secretary as I walked into the chemistry department office.

She, in return, politely greeted me. "Good morning, Joseph. You are ten minutes early. You may have to wait for a few minutes." She ushered me into his office. "He is in his laboratory with his research team. I will let him know that you are waiting for him." She walked back to her desk and left me in the inner office.

When Professor Ezir arrived for our meeting, he sat down without introducing himself. He probably assumed that I knew who he was. He sat behind his cluttered desk and lit his pipe. It was after his pipe was lit that he looked at me. "Joseph, I have heard so much about your acade-mic excellence from my students and faculty," he said.

"Thank you for the compliment, Professor Ezir," I replied.

"My goal is to show you what we do in this department that may be of benefit to you in the future. We have sev-eral research programs available for outstanding students like you. It is better for you to identify a faculty member early that may serve as your mentor." He stood up and took me on a tour of the research laboratories in the department.

His research laboratory was the first place we visited. He had several students and research assistants busy with their projects when we walked in. He walked over to a tall bespectacled student and asked her to take a short break in order to be introduced to me. "Gina, this is Joseph, the new student I talked to you about."

Gina was a graduate student chosen by Professor Ezir to be a student mentor for me. She was different from most of the students I'd met in school so far. She was tall, slim, and wore no makeup. However, I considered her beautiful and courteous. The most important aspect of our meeting was her first statement to me. "Joseph, I heard that you are smart, but it takes more than smarts to succeed in a science career." She apparently was not impressed by all the accolades that were prematurely bestowed on me. "I have seen smart students flunk out of this institution because of poor time management and laziness. I hope you will not become one of the statistics."

She was very passionate with her statements to me. She told me all the things to avoid if I was to make it in school. I felt filleted by her acerbic tongue as our conversation continued. At times, she sounded like a mother scolding her son. I must have walked into the laboratory with a swagger and a chip on my shoulder, which she felt compelled to knock off before it was too late.

It was apparent to me why Professor Ezir chose Gina to be my student mentor. "Thank you, Gina, for your good advice. I study hard every day, and I do not consider myself a lazy student."

She smiled for the first time. "I am very sorry, Joseph. I did not mean to sound harsh." She tactfully apologized after she got her points across to me.

When I turned around, I realized that Professor Ezir had left. It was hard to tell if he heard some of Gina's comments. "Gina, do I need to go back to Professor Ezir's office?" I said to her as I walked away from her laboratory.

She thought about it for a while, then said, "Probably. On your way out, stop by to say goodbye to him. He is a very good person, and you should feel privileged that he wants you to work with him."

It was the first time I'd heard that he wanted me to work with his research group. I tempered my exuberance to avoid further scolding from Gina.

"Joseph, I expect you to stop by my laboratory once a week to report on your academic progress. You also have the privilege to use the departmental library for your studies on week days."

I could not imagine why I needed to report weekly to Gina. I later found out from the departmental secretary that Gina was the best student who'd ever graduated from the department. She'd graduated from the school with the highest honors ever given to a student.

# # #

It appeared that the freedom I celebrated and cherished when I left home dissipated like morning dew at sunrise.

I found it troubling at the time that my life was indirectly controlled by so many women. I was studying daily with Wendy and Lisa by their request. Apart from studying together, Wendy had also requested that we have lunch together on week days.

"Joseph, you are the only person I can discuss academic issues with comfortably. I need you to motivate me to study for my medical school admission test. I have so much to cover and feel that I am falling behind," Wendy said to me before we started studying together. I could not turn her request down, and fortunately I gained tremendously from the association. In the process of helping her, I improved my science knowledge base. Wendy and I became inseparable out of academic necessity, but we also supplemented the growth of our friendship with occasional free-spirited journeys when weather permitted.

Although Lisa and Wendy were very close friends, they came from different backgrounds. Lisa came from a blue collar family but was very proud of her heritage. My friendship with Lisa was very superficial but rewarding to me. She typed all my required class reports without remuneration. Since she turned down all the payment offers I made to her, I bought gift cards for her, which she also refused to accept. "Joseph, I do not need your money. You are struggling as much I am, and you need to save your money for needed school supplies," Lisa said to me after she turned down my gift. I tried to limit what she did for me because I was uncomfortable taking up her needed study time.

Lisa had a boyfriend, Bruce, who was a junior my freshman year. He was a football player who rarely studied. He was a free spirit and did not want his time to be constrained by rigorous academic pursuit. Although Bruce went out with us occasionally, I had difficulty relating to him. Some considered Bruce a good old boy, but I found him to be vulgar most of the time. He frequently called me names that were not flattering. He was unhappy that Lisa spent as much time as she did with me and Wendy. Bruce would have been called a bigot by some, but I felt that he did not know any better.

# # #

Two days before Thanksgiving break, Wendy came up with a new request. "Joseph, I told my parents that you are coming home with me for Thanksgiving. I hope you would not think that I am being too forward with you." She felt that I should spend the Thanksgiving break with her family so that I would not be alone in the dormitory.

Although we had grown closer, I did not feel comfortable accepting her offer. "Wendy, I have plans to catch up with my studies during the short break. I am very sorry that I cannot accept your offer."

She looked at me very intensely as I spoke to her. As I watched her face, it appeared that my answer wiped away her beautiful smile and unflatteringly stretched her dimpled cheeks. I'd made a big blunder with my answer, but it was too late to redress my mistake.

As time passed, and the silence between us became unbearable, Wendy finally mustered the courage to address me again. She was back to being Wendy; beautiful and kind. "Joseph, you will be all alone in the dormitory, missing out in the fun and fellowship with my family."

I hugged her very tightly as tears rolled down her cheeks. It was the best response to her statement at that time, because no words could have conveyed my sincere gratitude.

When her tears stopped flowing, appropriate words were no longer hard to come by. "Wendy, I am honored that you consider me worthy to spend a holiday with your family. I hope you were not offended because I did not accept your offer."

She giggled. "Joseph, I have grown very fond of you. I was afraid that I would miss you over the Thanksgiving holiday."

I was surprised by her confessional speech, which was laden with emotion and humility. Wendy tried a different approach to entice me to go home with her. She was very specific about the size of turkey they cooked each year, side dishes that filled half of their dining table, and her mother's baking.

I waited until she was done before I finished what I wanted to say. "Wendy, holidays are for family get togethers, not a time to bring home a lonely foreigner."

She feigned a smile. "You take good care of yourself, Joseph. Have a happy Thanksgiving." We hugged before she left me.

# # #

On Wednesday, the day before Thanksgiving, Wendy left school after her examinations were over. By sundown, I was the only student left in my dormitory floor. The noisy hallways became hollow, and the once bustling recreational room was empty. I kept busy doing my laundry and arranging my room. I also wrote letters to all my friends. I went to bed early and fell asleep reading a boring novel. On Thursday morning I watched the New York City Thanksgiving parade on television. When I became hungry, I could not find a place that was open to buy food. I had to settle for vending machine snacks. I missed my family terribly, and I cried when I thought about my mother, who probably missed her son. It was gratifying going through my family photographs.

On Friday morning, I was still in bed when my room intercom woke me up. "Good morning, Joseph. This is Christina at the reception desk. You have a visitor at the lobby."

It was very early in the morning, and I could not imagine who was left at school that had an interest in visiting me. "Thank you, Christina. Tell my guest that I will be down shortly." I brushed my teeth and washed up before going down to the lobby to see my guest.

Wendy was standing by the reception desk with a smile on her face. She was unusually bashful as I approached the reception desk, but she managed to hug me. Initially it was a light hug, then she held me as tight as she could. She planted gentle kisses all over my neck and cheeks. Her lips finally found mine and behaved as if they'd found a playground. It was only natural that emotionally laden words followed. "I missed you, Joseph. I could not sleep nor eat, worrying about you. I could not bear the thought of you being alone on Thanksgiving Day." It was tears of joy that betrayed the honesty of the moment. She waited for a comment from me, but I was not sure what to say. I was happy to see her, but I was not ready to surrender my emotions. It felt like a lifetime before she finally loosened her grip. She held my hands, giggling.

"Joseph, do you mind giving me a hand? I have few things in the car for you," Wendy said to me after her excitement was contained. We walked outside while holding hands. The passenger side of her sports car was loaded with neatly bagged food items. She'd brought every type of special food served by her mother for me to sample. She brought so much food that I needed to refrigerate some. Since I had no refrigerator in my room, Wendy promised to store perishable food items in her refrigerator. The baked goods stayed with me and would not last for more than a day.

I was overwhelmed by her generosity. "Thank you, Wendy, for thinking about me when you could have been with your family. I had missed you, too. I wanted to call you but could not find your home telephone number."

As I reminded her that she gave up her family to be with me, she sobbed uncontrollably. It was obvious that she wanted me to console her, but I was afraid that things were moving too fast between us. Falling in love, if that was what had happened to Wendy, without declaring being in love, created an awkward situation for us. I was very careful how I consoled Wendy. Although she occasionally violated the boundaries of our friendship, I was very careful not to tread in that direction without proper invitation.

"Wendy, how long do you plan stay with me?" I wanted to know so that I could plan things for us to do.

"Joseph, I am back in school to be with you. I am not going back home. Thanksgiving is over for me. We can do things together."

I had only inquired how long she was staying for the day. "Wendy, are you sure that giving up your family time is wise? I have nothing to offer you. All I do is eat, sleep and read."

She pondered for a while, then said, '"We can go to the local mall and see a movie. You don't need to entertain me, Joseph."

I was worried about her resolve. She appeared very determined to rough it out with me for two days and could not be dissuaded. "I am happy to have you with me, Wendy. I will forever be grateful for your friendship."

I found the jaunt to the mall with Wendy rewarding. We talked about my middle class family background and our families' financial disparity. "Wendy, do you like me because you feel sorry for me?" I asked during our discussion.

"Joseph, I am offended by your comment. Why should I feel sorry for you? Are you physically challenged?"

It was apparent that I offended her. "I did not mean to offend you, Wendy. I am just surprised that a rich beautiful girl like you wants to be with me."

She was furious when she spoke again. "Joseph, you love to hear me complement you. So here is your complement. You are handsome, smart, and a boatload of fun to be with. That is the truth, Joseph, and I am also crazy about you."

Kindness was a word I had used several times in my life, but I never fully understood its meaning until I met Wendy. She was kind to me in every way imaginable. She took risks for me and did not care what others thought about our odd friendship. Our ethnic and cultural differences were glaringly evident to everyone except to Wendy. We had insurmountable socioeconomic differences that could have discouraged many, but not her. She accepted me as a friend with all my shortcomings and told me several times that she felt privileged to know me. She made me aware of all the taunting she was subjected to by her friends because of me. They were eager to point out our socioeconomic differences and how things could not work out between us. We had a quasi-liaison that never amounted to a love affair, but her friends thought that we were romantically involved. She never felt the need to correct their wrong assumptions.

Apart from the constant negative peer pressure she was subjected to, she also had to listen to her parents about how wrong our close friendship was. Her father, according to Wendy, was very critical about our friendship and once asked her, "Of all the boys in school, why Joseph?"

She was honest with him about her feelings. "Daddy, he makes me happy," was what Wendy told her father. He made unflattering comments about me to Wendy, who took offense to it.

I was unhappy that I caused disaffection between Wendy and her father. "Wendy, your family comes first before me," was what I told her. I tried to avoid a situation where she had to choose between our friendship and her family, but apparently I had no control over such issues.

Wendy cried a lot on Friday night. We were at the student center alone for hours talking about our friendship for the first time. She had been subjected to verbal abuse by her friends since we met. I was ethnically different, and they felt that I should not be welcomed as one of them. Stories she told me were painful to her. "Joseph, I was ridiculed by my so-called friends because I care about you. Some of them stopped talking to me because they are narrow-minded. I asked them to get to know you first before they judge you." As she spoke, her tears flowed freely as if they were a measure of the level of her pain. Wendy was in an emotional turmoil that manifested physically. She could not even make eye contact with me as her story progressed.

It was obvious to me that she could not bear further torment from her established friends. There were no pretenses or colorful words left between us to cover up reality. I had no other choice but to offer her a way out of her misery. "Wendy, I can stay away from you, if it could make things better."

She turned toward me, with tears still flowing. "Joseph, I could not bear the thought of losing our friendship. I am disappointed that you are willing to give up on us."

Her statement was a big surprise to me. "So there is an 'us', Wendy?" I joked.

She grabbed my shirt collar and yanked me around while smiling for the first time since we came to the student center. Her eyes glowed, and her dimples became more prominent than ever. She gave me a light hug. "Thank you for understanding me, Joseph."

I ruffled her hair, which she protested. "I will always be your friend," I reassured her.

On Saturday we toured Wendy's favorite places. We were at the mall where she shopped for a brown leather jacket and silver bangles. The only thing I thought she was in love with at that time was her silver jewelry. Her silver bangles and necklaces were her trademark in school. I tried to talk her out of buying more jewelry, since she had more than she needed. She agreed with me initially until she found a bangle she "could not leave behind." She sounded as if she was on a rescue mission for fancy jewelry.

As we walked from one store to another, we heard mean comments people made about us, which we ignored. On one occasion she said, "I am ashamed of the prejudice common in this part of my country. Europe may be a better place for a mixed couple" I did not bother to ask her if we were a couple.

Although the special time we shared together during the Thanksgiving break brought us closer, it inadvertently exposed all the weaknesses we had. As Thanksgiving holiday came to an end, it appeared that Wendy decided to slow things down between us. She complained that I had been difficult to get to know and that I was not willing to express my feelings. I was mired in fears of inadequacy and could not commit to an exclusive relationship with Wendy. I knew that I could not afford to dine out as much as she did, and I was not willing to depend on her generosity.

Wendy was also affected by the onslaught of peer pressure and her family's unmitigated rejection of our friendship. She probably felt that the best way to solve her problem was to avoid direct contact with me. She stopped showing up for noon lunches and cancelled her subscription to our library study cubicle. In class, she sat at the rear and hurriedly left at the conclusion of lectures. We unabatedly drifted apart by her choice. There were no further discussions or compromises negotiated between us. Our quasi-relationship ended without fanfare, as if we were a withered rose that had lost aesthetic value. Our problems were compounded by the facts that I was too proud to beg her to reconsider her decision, and she was very disappointed that I did not see the need to offer my emotional surrender.

There was no goodbye from Wendy before she left for Christmas vacation. It was a terrible way to end a good friendship. I was disappointed with the sudden change in her behavior and the way she dealt with challenges posed by our friendship. However, I refused to embrace dejection. On December 20th, I received a letter from Wendy.

My Dearest Joe:

I am very sorry for the pain I might have caused you. You could not offer me love the way I wanted you to, and I was on the verge of losing my family because of you. I had to make hard decisions before I became insane. My father felt betrayed by me because of our friendship. He did not believe that we were just friends after I unexpectedly left home during Thanksgiving break. I was not completely honest with him, and you. I had strong feelings for you but did not know how to express it. You were always aloof with me, and I was afraid of being rejected by you. Several times I wanted your emotional and physical surrender but had to settle for your tease. It was therefore difficult for me to continue to pursue an unfulfilling friendship with you.

I know that you are alone in the dormitory, since you did not see the need to go home to your parents for Christmas break. I wish there was something I could have done for you. I hope you are not as lonesome as I am without you.

My father does not approve of us seeing each other in school. Although my mother supports our friendship, she had to side with my father. I am very sorry Joe, but I have to respect my parents' wishes. I miss seeing you, and being with you, but I have to stay at home. I thought about driving to school to see you, but that would break my father's heart. It was easier when I saw you in school every day, but now I am here all alone. I have your picture on my wall, with a caption below it; 'Joe, my dream chaser'. Please don't ask me what it means, because I won't tell you.

Make sure you find time to eat. I hope to see you when I get back to school in January, if I could muster the courage to come and visit you.

Forgive your weak friend.

Wendy.

P.S. I miss you, and I miss our friendship.

Chapter 7

When school reopened in January, I had no classes with Wendy, and I only saw her once during registration. She was polite but distant. "Hello, Joseph. How was your Christmas break?" Wendy said to me, as if she was obligated to speak to me.

I was not sure how to answer her question. I had a terrible time spending Christmas alone in the school dormitory, because I had nowhere to go. "Wendy, your letter was very comforting to me. Thank you for being kind and considerate. I am very sorry for my selfish ways."

She smiled and walked away. I felt that I was very sarcastic and that she was offended by my comment.

In February, I met four South African students during a general conference on international relations. They had escaped from South Africa apartheid and were brought to central North Carolina to study. I learned from them the meaning of world citizenship. They'd escaped from their country because of torture and political imprisonment. They were not able to obtain South African passports and were issued United Nations passports.

Sunny was a tall lanky fellow from a middle-class family. His crime was unauthorized mobilization of college students against the South Africa apartheid government. He was arrested during a secret meeting of his group. He was not aware that one of the students he recruited was an informant for the apartheid government. The informant had taped their previous meeting and provided it to a local police department. In the parlance of South Africa underground movement at the time, "I was compromised by my brother," Sunny said. He cried when he narrated their ordeal in a maximum security prison in South Africa. "They beat us daily and subjected us to electric shocks." He had scars from the torture he endured. It was shocking to see all the scars from daily floggings and high voltage electric burns. Although the scars had healed, his emotional pains lingered on. You could hear it in his cry, and you could feel the pain he felt, if you looked closer at the scars left behind on his back.

None of the three females talked about their experiences in prison and refugee camp. Sunny, however, was not restrained as he expressed his anger about the lack of respect and the loss of human dignity in the hands of their tormentors. "Joseph, I have nightmares daily. I still hear the cry of women being raped in the open by prison guards. I still hear their sobbing after they were raped. I still see them hiding their faces because of shame. It has been a nightmare for me since I left the South Africa prison."

I was moved by their experiences. We held hands together and prayed to God for deliverance of those still incarcerated for their political opinion in South Africa. "Sunny, help me to start a campus awareness program on South Africa struggles," I said to him. My emotional meltdown that day started an antiapartheid campus organization that marched on campus daily for months to inform interested students of the plight of South African blacks. It resulted in our university revoking its investments in South African Krugerrands in the mid -1970s.

On the first Saturday in February, I attended a campus religious revival with my South African friends. We arrived at the lecture hall where the revival was held five minutes before it started. Although students arrived in groups, they were somnolent. It was not hard to tell that it was a religious program because gregarious students became very reflective as they walked in. I was a staunch Catholic who attended Catholic church services regularly and was not prepared for what went on that day. We were sitting down listening to the singing when the preacher walked in. As soon as the preacher ascended to the podium, the tempo of singing increased. Spontaneous freestyle dancing erupted as the tempo of music rose. I sat still in my chair as a cacophony of mumbled sounds filled the hall.

The preacher interrupted the singing occasionally with, "Hallelujah! Hallelujah!" As he bellowed out "hallelujah" in rapid succession, the singing stopped. He read a chapter from the scripture while the audience clapped and danced. He stopped reading the chapter abruptly and started speaking in tongues. Everyone in the hall spoke in tongues and fell on the ground gyrating, except for me. I was the only one standing, and I felt embarrassed.

When they regained their natural senses, I asked Sunny what had happened to them. "Sunny, how was it possible that I was the only one who was not possessed by the Holy Spirit during your incantations?"

He looked at me, puzzled. "So Joseph, you did not feel the Holy Spirit?"

His statement was very comical to me, but I tried to hide my amusement. "No Sunny, I was not possessed. Maybe I am not holy enough to feel the spirit."

He ignored me as the program continued. He was still puzzled when he finally gave his true opinion to me. "You probably are not a true believer."

He was probably right. How could I believe in something that excluded me from the rest? There was no further need for me to stay with the chosen ones. I exited the hall and was welcomed by a biting, cold, windy February night. "Every nonbeliever has to be punished," I muttered to myself.

I shared my new religious experience with my mother when I wrote to her. Her reply was not encouraging. "My dearest son: I had warned you several times to stay away from religious zealots." She did not have to warn me anymore, because I thought it was despicable to fake a trance just to get attention. I was completely done with campus religious revivals. And although I shared with my family all the new experiences I had in school, I left Wendy out of my policy of open communication. I felt it was too personal to discuss my dalliance with a quasi amour.

# # #

The second semester was a busy time for me. Time went very fast, as I had wished. I avoided the central university library and, instead, studied in the chemistry library. Occasionally, I ventured into the law school library, since it stayed open 24 hours a day except for Sundays, when it closed at midnight. I had no social life and did not want one. I was afraid to make new friends because of the mess I got Wendy into with her family. I felt that I should learn more about the culture of my new country, rather than delve into complex friendships. My weekly meeting with Gina became educational sessions on culture and etiquette. I learned as much as I could from Gina, who had no social life herself. Some of my questions to Gina on dating and relationships made her laugh. She was curious about my sudden preoccupation with love and relationships.

"Joseph, I would like to know who your love interest is. It appears that you may be infatuated with someone on campus." She was surprised when I told her that I was not seeing anyone at that time. She probably did not believe me. "How about the girl that followed you around last year? She has long golden hair, dimples, and always carries a red bag."

I was surprised at the detailed physical description of Wendy. "I was not aware that you were spying on me," I told her.

"Joseph, in a small campus, some people stand out. You have to know that a lot of people watch what you do here." She did not elaborate on why I stood out, and I did not want to know.

In late April, I was notified of my nomination to a national honors society. I was also nominated by my department for three scholarship awards and by two other departments for outstanding freshman student. I wondered if Wendy was getting awards too, since she was an excellent student. I was tempted to contact her to find out, but I was afraid to reopen a closed line of communication between us.

The school awards day was a big event that took place a few days before the academic year ended in May. It was a hot May afternoon, and I was apprehensive about my unbridled state of profuse sweating, when I walked into the basketball gymnasium where the awards ceremony was held. The first person that I made eye contact with was Wendy, and she beckoned me to sit next to her. It would have been awkward if I refused. She was flanked by Lisa and Francesca, who waved at me. As I approached their row, Francesca stood up and walked over to Lisa's side to create an empty space for me next to Wendy. My preference was to sit away from Wendy, because I was still sweating and was very self-conscious.

"Hello Wendy, Lisa, Francesca," I said to the sorority friends as Wendy motioned for me to sit down next to her. As soon as I sat down, she whispered in my ear, "I have missed you terribly, Joseph."

It was not the right place and situation to go into personal matters. I merely smiled at her and did not say anything.

"Joseph, how many awards are you getting today?" Lisa asked.

"I am not sure, Lisa." I said. I tried very hard to stop all the attention I was getting. All I wanted at that time was for my sweating to stop.

I was going through the pages of the awards pamphlet attentively when Wendy touched my knee to get my attention. "Joseph, I am the one who nominated you for the national scientific honor society. I feel that you are the best student in academics and moral character in this institution. You therefore deserve all the accolades you will be accorded today."

I reached out, held her hand, and squeezed gently, and she reciprocated. When I looked up, I could see tears in her eyes. Lisa and Francesca stood up and walked away. They probably felt that we needed our privacy.

"I am very sorry, Joseph, for how I treated you," she said to me.

"Wendy, it was not my intention to become a burden for you," I said as she wiped her tears.

She feigned a smile, before she spoke. "I have never met anyone like you, Joseph. You filled my life with joy, and then they took it away from me." Her words sounded very sincere, and I could feel her pain, too. We had an upper torso embrace at the same time Lisa and Francesca walked back to their chairs.

Francesca looked at us and smiled. "Have you two kids made up?" Francesca said. Her question was very sarcastic, so she did not get any answer from me.

When the program started, we did not speak again. The president of the university led us in a prayer before he announced the awards. "Parents, professors, and students, we have a unique situation this year. The best freshman student awards in chemistry, biology, mathematics, and philosophy are going to one outstanding student."

The hall erupted in claps and whistles. The hall was still noisy when my name was called. The only thing I heard because of the noise was "Joseph ... please come up to the podium to receive your awards."

My last name was probably hard for him to pronounce, so he barely said it. Wendy hugged me so hard that I quit breathing for a second. When she let go of me, I walked up to the podium with tears of joy flowing freely. The noise generated by the audience was so loud that it continued to reverberate even when the cheering stopped. I accepted my awards gleefully and walked back to my chair.

The next awardee was Wendy, who was recognized in biology and chemistry for the sophomore class.

After we received our awards, Wendy handed me a piece of paper with her home address and telephone number. She requested that I keep in touch during the summer vacation. She had plans to go to New York and the south of France for the summer. She left school the following day without saying goodbye.

I did not hear from Wendy until I received a letter from her dated May 31.

Hello again! ☺

I just returned home from New York. I had a nice trip! I went shopping, and I went to see The Wiz!

Joseph, it was nice spending time with you in school. I miss talking to you. You were one of the few people I had the pleasure of knowing who had something constructive to talk about. I am also glad that I have your picture on my wall!

You were right when you told me to spend more time on my studies. My awards justified all the hard work I put into my studies .I deeply appreciate your support. One of my grades was awful. I made four A's and one B + . I would have been satisfied, but that was not the best I could have done. My overall average is still 3.85. I would like to come back to school for summer session, but my father wants me to have a regular summer vacation.

I hope I get to see you this summer. I would like to know you better! You are a wonderful person! Stay sweet and forever beautiful!

Love ya!!!

Wendy

P.S. I'll send you a picture when they come back from the photo shop.

I read Wendy's letter several times and was more confused than before. The agony of trying to figure out what Wendy wanted was unbearable. My freshman communication lecture was applicable at this juncture. We were instructed to be careful how we interpreted spoken and written words. I decided not to read too much into Wendy's letter. I took it as a letter from a close friend. I did not analyze the letter as much as I should have. I did not reply to her letter, because I was confused about her intention. We were probably two confused teenagers who had difficulty understanding adult-type relationships and societal prejudices. I sincerely believed that she was presented with the option of being my friend with the total loss of her family financial support or staying away from me with the benefit of complete financial support from her family. Whatever was the truth, I never faulted her decision.

Wendy did not come back for summer school, as she said in her letter. On the first of June, I moved into a university apartment and started my summer research job. I was allowed to register for a class in theoretical chemistry while working as a research assistant. It was a challenging class that occupied all the available time I had.

I had daily contact with Gina during the summer session, which was very helpful to me. Although we had different research projects, she made time to guide me in new research techniques. In spite of my indifference to friendship, Gina was very caring and was very concerned about my wellbeing. She told me frequently that I was her little brother. "Good morning my little brother Joseph," she would say to me every morning.

My response was equally comical; "Good morning to you too, my big sister Gina." We worked well together throughout the summer. She asked questions about my social life, and always received the same answer from me. "I have no social life Gina. I am just a foreign student trying to survive in your country." She would laugh at my silliness.

In late July, Gina invited me to accompany her family to an amusement park. She was elated when I accepted her invitation. Since I had not met her family, she spent some time describing everyone for me.

"My father is the silent type," Gina said. "My mother, my brother Brian, and my sister Maria are easy to get to know. My sister Debbie is a different story." She was very exhaustive with each family member personality except for Debbie. "My sister Debbie is so different from everyone in my family that my father joked about his real daughter being switched in the hospital after birth. Debbie asked my father several times to return her to her rightful parents." It appeared that Gina had a very loving family and a father with good sense of humor.

I accepted Gina's invitation to accompany her family to an amusement park. They planned a short trip to a western North Carolina mountain town. The long trip to this "ghost town in the sky" with Gina's family was a memorable one. I was picked up from my apartment by Gina very early in the morning. Her father was worried about daytime high temperatures so he requested an early morning departure. His decision was also affected by the fact that their van had no air conditioning. When we arrived at their house, her father was busy cleaning the inside of their van. He was so preoccupied with his cleaning that he barely said hello to me when we arrived. I was worried that he might have been unhappy that I was invited to travel with them.

"Mr. Myer, do you mind if I help you clean the van?" I said. Cold sweat drenched my undershirt, and my heart fluttered as I waited for an answer after my offer to help. I waited for more than five minutes before I gained the courage to ask again if he would mind my assistance. Since he ignored me again, I changed the conversation. "I am very grateful for your generosity," I said with my voice quivering. I wondered what I meant by generosity. It was the only word that I could think of under duress.

It felt like a lifetime before he looked at me and smiled. "Gina is a good kid and knows how to pick good friends," he said. "You are welcome to my house any time."

His wife joined us before he could finish his sentence. Gina's mother hugged me when we were introduced. She was a pleasant woman and probably a good mother to her children. "How do you cope with being away from your family for so long, Joseph?" she asked me.

I reassured her that I was used to being away from home. Gina, Brian, Debbie, and Maria walked to their mother's side as our conversation continued.

When he finished cleaning the van, Mr. Myer interrupted their mother to give instructions to Brian about sitting in the back row with me, while the three girls sat in the middle row. I followed Brian to sit in the last row without hesitation. I was relieved with the seating assignment, because I could not imagine sitting very close to the girls while their father's probing eyes watched me with suspicion. Brian was a jolly fellow who kept me laughing with his unending tales.

We sat peacefully in our rows until we left their house. "Joseph, how do you like our college town?" their mother asked.

Brian was waiting for me to give an honest assessment of their town when Debbie interrupted me. "Joseph likes our town because Gina is keeping him happy, if you know what I mean." Debbie's comment was very provocative, but it failed to elicit a reaction from Gina. If her parents heard what she said they ignored it, as I did.

"Brian, I may come over to your row when we stop, because Gina is boring. Maybe I will sit on Joseph's lap and see what Gina would do about it," Debbie provocatively said.

Their parents were engaged in a serious conversation and were not paying close attention to the events in the rear seats. When Debbie realized that I was uneasy about her comments, she taunted me more. Her siblings ignored her, and I was left to suffer in silence. Debbie was vulgar at times, which infuriated Gina. I could not frown nor smile as Debbie carried on with her playful invasion of my private space. When she reached behind and touched my legs, Gina spanked her hand. They had a minor scuffle, which ended when their parents scolded them about their immaturity and lack of respect. After the scolding by their parents, they stared at each other with visible anger. I was uneasy the rest of the drive to the amusement park.

The amusement park was nestled on a beautiful mountain in western North Carolina. We drove through several winding hillside roads until we arrived at the foothills, where we boarded the ski lifts that took us up the mountain. Gina's parents were afraid of heights and opted for a train ride up the hill. I rode with Gina, while Brian rode with Debbie. Debbie protested riding with Brian. "Gina, are you afraid that I would make out with Joseph if we rode together?" Debbie asked Gina. I pretended that I did not understand what she meant by making out with me.

"I may let Joseph ride me like a pony today," Debbie continued with her vulgarity.

"Debbie, I am not a cowboy. Even if I was a cowboy, why should I settle for a pony instead of a real horse?" I said to her.

My comment drew laughter from Gina and Brian. Debbie patted my back with a grin and ran to her lift.

# # #

The aerial view from the lift was spectacular. We had 360 degrees of unimpeded view of the county. There were multiple hills in the horizon, separated by valleys covered with pine trees. I was so intrigued with the view that I forgot my fear of heights. Graciously, Gina pointed out all the surrounding towns to me and their economic importance to the state. Her family had visited the park every year since she was five years old. When she was done with her civic lecture, she apologized to me about Debbie's behavior. "Joseph, my sister was not trying to offend you. I think she likes you but does not know how to express her feelings."

My smile gave away my feelings. I reassured her that I was not offended but rather found it amusing. I asked Gina before we disembarked from the lift about her future plans after graduate school. She was candid with me for a change.

"I stayed behind to do graduate work because my fiancée did not graduate with his class. He did not finish one of his required courses. However, I have an admission to a medical school in Florida for the next academic year." She walked closer to me and said, "My family will always be here for you if you need them." She turned to Debbie and said, "I take Joseph as our brother. You have to look after him when I leave for Florida in one month. You should not take advantage of his good nature." Debbie, with teary eyes, apologized to me for misbehaving in the van.

We spent the rest of the day enjoying what the "ghost town in the sky" had to offer.

# # #

On the 10th of August, Gina left for medical school. She left me a simple note in my research laboratory.

Joseph,

Try always to do your best in school. Do not get distracted while I am gone. I hope to see you when I come home for Thanksgiving. I will miss our weekly arguments. Stay sweet always.

Gina.

A few days after Gina left for Florida, I sent her a postcard to show my appreciation.

To my sister Gina:

I promise not to disappoint you. I registered for my classes this morning and will devote my time studying. I am taking physics, applied mathematics, organic chemistry, microbiology, and scientific instrumentation. I am very grateful for all you did for me. I do cherish our closeness. Please keep in touch.

Joseph.

Before the end of summer vacation, I was given credits for four courses I challenged. Some departments allowed students to challenge some introductory courses. I took and passed comprehensive examinations in the four courses and was awarded twelve credited hours. When the twelve credit hours were added to my transcript, the total number of credit hours I had qualified me as a junior at the start of my second year in school.

I had planned to see Wendy before we started classes on August 24, but unfortunately she did not come back to school until the night of August 23rd. She did not stop by to say hello to me after she returned to school. I was disappointed that she did not make any effort to see me. On the morning of August 24th, before I went to my first class, I left a note at her dormitory's reception desk. My note simply read:

Welcome back Wendy. My classes start at 8 am today. Meet me at the cafeteria at 12 noon for lunch. Joseph.

Fall 1978

Chapter 8

On the first day of fall semester, after a long summer session, I was surprised to see Francesca in my physics lecture hall. She smiled as we exchanged greetings. "How was your summer vacation Joseph?" she asked me attentively.

"I was in school for the summer," I said. It was the first time she had engaged in a lengthy conversation with me. She was physically fit, with eye-catching curves, pearly white teeth, golden curly hair, evenly tanned skin, and shoulders draped with a flowing white cotton dress. She had an air of a vacationing princess who was lost without her prince. Although she smiled at me, she had a worried look on her face.

I was compelled to ask if she was all right. "Francesca, you look very pensive. Is everything OK with you?"

She lowered her head before she answered me. "Joseph, physics has been a big worry for me since I enrolled in college five years ago. I need to complete the two classes before I can graduate in May." According to Francesca, she had spent five years in college because she changed her major twice. She was also busy with cheerleading and part-time modeling, which prevented her from registering for more than four classes per semester. She took the minimum required hours every semester to make time for her extracurricular activities.

As we waited for the professor to arrive, she continued to tell me her life story. She ran out of school grants after four years and had to pay for her fifth year out of pocket. She moved off campus to help save some money with her living expenses. She was still narrating her story when the physics professor walked in. We walked together to two empty seats and sat next to each other. I avoided eye contact with Francesca during the 50 minutes of lecture. I was in a hurry after the lecture, and I barely said goodbye to her because I had to walk to the chemistry building for my next lecture. She waved as I exited the lecture hall. I was not interested in her story and could not subject myself to any further insincere politeness.

I barely made it to the cafeteria before noon after my morning lectures. I was surprised to see Wendy waiting for me by the doorway of the cafeteria. I was extending my hand for a handshake when she hugged me. She apologized for being away in Europe without letting me know. She made the last-minute decision to join her family in the south of France after she sent me a letter.

"I am so happy to see you back in school, Wendy. I missed you a lot." Before I could finish what I was saying, she reached out and held my hand. We walked into the cafeteria and searched for a quiet place to sit down. We could not find a private table after an exhaustive search in all corners of the cafeteria and finally settled for a table with four students. She declined an offer from me to get her lunch. I walked to the lunch line and bought some snacks. I sat directly in front of Wendy, who watched me eat. She spent 30 minutes watching me eat alone and could not stop talking about her summer vacation. I had nothing to tell her about my summer vacation except for the "ghost town in the sky."

"Joseph, I regret not asking you to go to the south of France with me."

It was hard to tell if she was sincere about her regret. However, I quipped, "Wendy, you knew I could not have accepted your offer since I have limited financial resources."

She looked at me intently and said, "Joseph, are you trying to tell me that I am not capable of taking care of you for a month in Europe?"

I found myself on the defensive, trying to explain to her that it would be unreasonable for me to accept such an offer. When she realized that I was getting uncomfortable with the discussion, she asked about my physics class with Francesca. I was surprised that she knew about my physics class.

She watched the puzzled look on my face and said, "Francesca came by my room after your class ended this morning. She was excited to see you in her class. I hope you will help her with physics."

I told Wendy that I would try to help Francesca develop good study habits. I was not sure how Francesca studied and was only making an assumption that she did not study as much as Wendy did. As our conversation progressed, I realized that Wendy and Francesca had been good friends for a long time. However, they had not seen much of each other lately because of Francesca's modeling engagements. Wendy was not the type of person who would criticize others when they were not present, so she said that she would reserve further comments on Francesca until she could formally introduce her to me.

I wondered why Francesca needed a special introduction to me, but did not say much. Wendy was properly schooled in social diplomacy and was always appropriate. She was not the type of person who would hurt her friends' feelings, but she was always forthright with those close to her. These were the attributes of Wendy that I admired. It was, therefore, surprising to me that she was reluctant to discuss with me what went wrong with our friendship. I felt that she was trying to avoid hurting my feelings with unchecked sincerity.

"See you around, Joseph," Wendy said to me as she was about to leave for her next class.

"Are you not studying with me tonight, Wendy?" I said.

"I had assumed that you are going to study with Francesca, since you are taking physics together," she said to me.

I was puzzled by her statement and could not say anything further. "Let's keep in touch, Wendy," was the only thing I could say before I walked away. She tried to say something to me before I walked away, but apparently felt that what she had to say could wait. As I walked away, Wendy stood where I left her. I turned around and walked back to her. I was surprised that she had tears in her eyes.

"Joseph, I am very sorry about the way I have treated you lately. I have been taunted by my friends about our friendship, and I could not bear it any more."

I was moved by her honesty and apologized for unknowingly making her life miserable. I promised to keep away from her if that would make her happy. She assured me that she valued our friendship but needed time to sort things out. I jokingly asked what she expected from her friends when she spent all her time with a foreigner.

"Look at us, Wendy, vanilla and cocoa, trying to be close friends in a small university town under the watchful eyes of our peers." She laughed uncontrollably and asked me how I came up with our nicknames, vanilla and cocoa. "I could not find better words to describe two misfits," I said to her as I walked away while she was still laughing.

Chapter 9

I was standing by a workstation in the physics laboratory when Francesca walked in. It was our first laboratory session. She walked in with her typical air of confidence and the rhythmic motion of a seasoned majorette. I took my time to look her over for the first time. Her hair was perfectly done, and she wore green eye shadow to accentuate her green eyes. Her pink tank top was partially covered by a small white cotton shirt. She had on a fitted pair of white jean pants that accentuated her perfect figure and a pair of white sandals. She walked straight to my location and asked if she could be my laboratory partner. She sat down next to me before she finished her request. She probably knew that I could not say no to her.

Most of the students were noticeably distracted, since they were staring at us. They spoke to each other in hushed voices, but some of the things they said could be heard by Francesca. I was surprised by some of the racially insensitive names they called me.

"She must be looking for a pet monkey and found one in school," was one of the comments I heard from one of the boys. While some of the men admired Francesca's bold demeanor, the women looked at her with disgust out of jealousy.

"Joseph, ignore those boys. They are jealous of you. You are smart, handsome, and have a beautiful accent." Her words were so seductive that I lost interest in what was being said about me. She twirled my name with her tongue in an exaggerated North Carolina accent. She was purposefully seducing me with words as her face beamed with a mischievous smile. I had to quickly disengage from her hypnotic eyes.

"I am in trouble," I muttered under my breath.

When our physics laboratory class started, I focused on the project assigned for the day. I took college-level physics in high school and had already done the project we were given. One of the students who'd called me racial names came over to apologize when he realized that I knew how to set up the experiment we were assigned. I tried to be gracious and pretend as if I was not offended by their earlier remarks. I was there for my education and not to redress sociocultural inequities. I helped as many students as possible to set up their experiments.

"I am very proud of you, Joseph. You did not show any sign of malice toward the boys who verbally abused you," Francesca said to me before the period ended.

I had to remind her that I did not have many options, since I was a guest in her country. "How could I be angry when I have the most beautiful girl on campus sitting next to me?" I said to her.

Francesca's face was beaming with a smile as I complimented her. She apparently was not expecting any flirtation from me. I was surprised by my forwardness and felt that her perfume might have affected my sanity.

I thought about my failed friendship with Wendy and felt nauseated about what was happening to me again in the physics laboratory. I resolved to keep away from Francesca. However, I agreed to be her study partner when she asked me. We agreed to meet at the library after dinner. "Francesca, you are aware that I am doing Wendy a favor by agreeing to study with you," I said to her.

She looked at me, perplexed. "Joseph, I thought you were my friend too." I could not disagree with her statement. To make up for my faux pas, I offered to walk Francesca back to her place of residence. She flirtatiously protested that we did not know each other that well. I was about to walk away when she changed her mind and handed over her books to me.

I did most of the talking as we walked on a path leading to the house where she lived. It was an old brick house with a poorly manicured hedge. The dry, hot summer had killed what was probably a scanty lawn. Although the outside of the house needed attention, the inside was well kept. The living room was decorated tastefully with antique furniture that included a display cabinet with painstakingly arranged crystals. Mrs. Thomas, who boarded Francesca, was sitting by her piano and flipping through a music book as we walked in. I was introduced as a classmate by Francesca. Mrs. Thomas thoroughly assessed me from head to toe.

"Hello, Mrs. Thomas, nice to meet you," I said as she continued to look me over thoroughly.

She adjusted her reading glasses many times before she stood up to shake my hand. "Where are you from, son?" I answered her question very promptly as Francesca stood by and watched. "I have never heard of your country," she said. I was rambling on about the economic importance of my country to America when she turned to Francesca to remind her of the house rules. She walked to her kitchen as if I was no longer there. I knew it was time for me to leave.

Francesca walked with me to the door and confirmed our study time for the evening. "See you at the library tonight, Joseph." She closed the door as I walked away.

# # #

I had to rush through early dinner before walking to the library at 5:45. I was very anxious about studying with Francesca. She was very personable, contrary to my initial impression of her. It surprised me that we got along well. I had expected her to be self-absorbed, but she turned out to be very attentive. It was evident that she was interested in what I had to say. She was so attentive that it worried me. I felt that she was not the type of student I should be spending my time with, since we did not have much in common. She was a beautiful, mature student and a model. I was certain that men begged her to go out with them. I took stock of what I had to offer Francesca, who was to graduate in a few months, and came up with nothing.

"Hello, Joseph. Do you have an assigned cubicle, or are we using general sitting places?" Francesca said to me.

I was happy that she arrived early to stop me from unnecessary self-assessment. We were meeting to study, and not for a date. "Hello, beautiful." I was shocked at what came out of my mouth.

"Oh! Thank you, Joseph." She blushed from my compliment. I was ashamed of what I said to her and avoided eye contact.

We found an empty study table at the far end of the library. I went over my study rules with Francesca before we started to study. She accepted my recommendation of two uninterrupted hours of study, followed by a 15-minute break. We sat across from each other rather than next to each other, which was a deviation from my previous stint with Wendy. It was difficult not to compare everything we did with what I did with Wendy.

I brought physics and chemistry books to study. She brought several books with her, which she spread on the desk. I realized early that she was having difficulty deciding what to study first. "Francesca, why don't we start with physics so that we can discuss it during our first break?"

She took my suggestion and opened her physics book to study. Although she concentrated on what she was reading initially, she spent a significant amount of time looking at me. I was uncomfortable and tried to avoid eye contact with her. I set goals every study period and was not willing to fail on my goals. When she realized that I was serious about my studies, she became serious, too.

During our 15-minute break, Francesca bluntly asked me, "Were you in love with my friend Wendy?"

Her question took me by surprise. I knew she would tell Wendy what I said about our friendship. I was not sure what she wanted to know, so I asked her for clarification. "Francesca, I am not sure what you mean by being in love. Can you be more specific on what you want to know?" I probably sounded ignorant, but it was necessary at that time.

"I want to know what happened between the two of you and why you are not close any more."

I was probably rambling when I began to answer her question. "I care about Wendy, but we were not romantically involved, as some people wrongly thought. We are not taking classes together this semester, so we don't get see each other as much as we used to." She wanted to know more about my relationship with Wendy, so I told her details of the special friendship we had.

"So, Joseph, you let her go without putting up a fight?" she scolded me.

"We are still friends, but we are not as close as we used be," I said to her. I told her about the taunting Wendy was exposed to because of me.

"Joseph, are you worried about what they may say about our friendship?" Francesca asked me. She smiled and told me that she did not care about what people had to say. "I like you, Joseph, and I want us to be friends. I need your help to pass physics and graduate in May." Francesca did not finish what she was saying when I told her that we had to go back and finish studying. "I can tell that you are shy, Joseph," she teased me. I smiled and avoided any further incriminating statements.

As we walked back to our study table, I was more aware of probing eyes around us. It was the puzzled look on their faces that gave away their inner thoughts. I guess it was not commonplace for a beautiful college majorette to be socially paired with a sociocultural outsider, which I felt was a good description of my status on campus. I tried not to reveal my uneasiness to all the peering eyes that followed us until we sat down to resume our studies. I suggested to Francesca that we should not take any more study breaks for the night.

# # #

Our campus was well lit by street lights at night, and we had good security. I was oblivious to any potential physical danger to me or my study companion. However, Francesca was aware of all the risks we faced while walking together at night. She recommended the law school library as a more secure place for our nightly study, rather than the main school library. "The law school library stays open 24 hours a day, and the students are more enlightened. It is probably more secure for us," she said to me.

When we finished studying for the night, Francesca was eager to leave the library. We had barely walked out of the library when she reached out and held my hand. Her action took me by surprise, and unfortunately my palm started to sweat. I was very nervous, and she had fun teasing me about it.

"Joseph, are you trying to show me that you never held hands with Wendy before?" I swallowed my saliva hard, and I was sure she heard it. "Can we walk to the student center building for ice cream?" she asked me. I agreed to walk with her to the student center. To my surprise, she did not let go of my hand when we walked into the building, which was packed with many students. Of all the people we could run into that night in my compromised situation, we ran into Wendy and Lisa, who were standing in line to be served.

Wendy whistled at us and said, "I left you guys alone for a day, and you are already holding hands."

I was very uncomfortable while holding Francesca's hand but could not do anything about it. Wendy left her place in line and walked over to us to chat. She looked at Francesca very sternly and said, "If you hurt Joseph in any way, you have to answer to me. He is genuinely sweet and innocent. You, my friend Francesca, I am not so sure of your intentions."

Francesca was speechless and smiled at Wendy. We sat down together after we were served. Interestingly, Wendy sat down next to me, while Lisa and Francesca were holding a conversation about their sorority event.

Wendy looked at me with concern on her face and said, "Joseph, I am happy for you, but I hope you know what you are getting yourself into. I do not want to see you get hurt."

I knew she meant well, but I felt that she was overly concerned. "I am very grateful for your concern, Wendy, but there is nothing going on between Francesca and me. I believe she was trying to be provocative, and I let it happen." I was not sure if Wendy felt betrayed by me or Francesca. I was remorseful and reassured Wendy that my social life would not affect our special friendship.

"Joseph, you may have a love affair with Francesca, but don't you ever let it affect our friendship."

Wendy was showing a possessive side that I never saw before. When I stood up to leave, Wendy hugged me hard and wished me good luck. The three sorority sisters waved goodbye to me as I walked away.

Chapter 10

I became more resilient after being away from home for so long. I considered myself independent and did not feel that I needed anyone. However, I was worried about the effect a demanding relationship would have on my academic pursuits. I was very ambitious and did not want anything to affect my goals. I maintained good study habits and only socialized with students who had a genuine interest in education. I worried constantly about disappointing my family. My father had no doubt about my dedication to academic excellence when I left home. He supported me immensely to enable me to achieve my goals. He was so sure of my moral goodness that nothing more was necessary to be said after he left me at the airport with only a few words. My mother, on the other hand, warned me, "Don't disappoint me, my son."

Although my parents did not have direct involvement with my daily life in school, my dedication to them still influenced everything I did. It was therefore not surprising that I agonized over Francesca. I wondered what my parents would say if they knew we were spending time together. I made a mental list of her positive and negative attributes. For each negative thing I thought about, I mimicked what my mother would have said about it. The negative things were mostly lifestyle issues that she had no control over. One thing that stood out was her parents' divorce. Although she had no control over their divorce, my mother would have felt uneasy about my association with someone from a broken home. It was one area I felt that my parents' opinion did not matter to me at that time. I stopped wasting my time pontificating about all the negative issues about Francesca, since I had no intention of telling my parents about her. Holding hands with Francesca did not amount to much, I finally concluded.

On the second Friday of the semester, I had a minor accident in the chemistry laboratory. I had gone into the laboratory to complete an organic chemistry experiment. I had an hour to spare before lunch, so I felt the need to use my time wisely. Francesca was to meet me in the chemistry building at noon so that we could go out to lunch. I was unaware that the ventilation hood directly above my workspace was malfunctioning.

Two graduate students, John and Melissa, were in the laboratory when I walked in. John was a Ph.D. student who loved teaching and helping undergraduate students. "Joseph, what brings you here at this time of the day?" John asked as soon as I walked into the laboratory. He joked about how successful he had been in turning me into a chemist. Melissa was shy, but personable. She was too busy fiddling with a spectroscopy machine.

As soon as I settled down to begin my work, I complained about their choice of radio station because the loud, hard rock music was affecting my concentration. I could not imagine how a student could think while such a ruckus was going on in a learning environment. "Hard rock makes my brain rock too, man," John drawled.

"John, that manner of speaking does not fit you. You pretend to be a rebel, but you are really a lab rat." I was barely done with my rebuke when he turned around, and simulated playing a guitar. I smiled at him and retreated to my work space.

I was almost done with my experiment when I felt a burning sensation in both of my eyes. I complained to John and Melissa about the burning sensation. They inspected my work area and concluded that my workspace air ventilation was not working. I used the eye wash sink in the laboratory for immediate first aid care, as stipulated by the laboratory guidelines. Although I rinsed my eyes thoroughly, they continued to burn when Francesca arrived to go with me to the cafeteria. My shirt was soaked with water, and it was evident that she was alarmed to see me in that state.

"I am very sorry about the way I look, Francesca. I was exposed to chemical fumes a few minutes ago and had to rinse my eyes."

She dismissed my apology as unnecessary but was rather concerned about my swollen red eyes. "You need to have your eyes checked. I feel that we should go to the emergency room now," she demanded.

She took me to the university hospital for proper evaluation. I could not open my eyes by the time we arrived at the emergency room. She helped me with the hospital registration and sat next to me while I waited to be seen. When my name was called, Francesca stood up, held my hand, and walked me to the examination room.

"Only next of kin are allowed in the examination room," the nurse said to Francesca.

"I am the only person he has locally," Francesca quipped.

The nurse walked away without further demands. The doctor that attended to me was more understanding and complimented Francesca for being a dedicated friend to me. He irrigated my eyes before he conducted a thorough examination. He applied some ointment in my eyes and patched them. I was instructed to keep the patches on for 24 hours. I was discharged with eye drops. Francesca walked me back to my apartment, which was less than a block away from the university hospital. I could only imagine the spectacle we made; a southern belle walking a blind foreign student home. My companion probably did not care.

My apartment was scantly decorated, and therefore did not pose much danger for me during my 24 hours of imposed blindness. I had a sofa, a chair, and a coffee table in my living room. My walls were barren, and I had few cooking utensils in the kitchen. It was a place where I slept and not a place for entertainment. A small television and a shortwave radio were the only things I had for entertainment.

Francesca found my refrigerator empty and was concerned. "Do you have money for food, Joseph?" she asked me. She was deeply concerned about my welfare. I told her that I did not have the need to buy food, since I ate at the school cafeteria. I left out the most interesting secret I had. I did not tell her that most of the meals I had in school were bought with Wendy's meal card. I had the money to buy food but did not want to waste my money when I had the option of free meals. Since Wendy did not eat at the school cafeteria, she gave me her meal cards every semester.

Francesca was done with her classes for the week and had no plans to go home for the weekend after she brought me back to my apartment. She voluntarily took up the job of caring for me. She made a grocery list with my assistance before she went to the nearest store. I dozed off after she left and was woken up from sleep by her knock on my door. I felt my way to the door to let her in. She brought her cassette player and placed it on the small dining table in the kitchen.

She cleaned the refrigerator and then unpacked what she bought. She also washed the unused dishes in the cabinets, utensils, and glassware. "I want to start off with a clean kitchen." She said.

Her statement did not go well with me. "Francesca, I was not aware that my kitchen was dirty."

Sensing that I was offended by her statement, she tried to appease me with an explanation for her action. "Your apartment is very clean, but clean dishes may need to be rewashed before they are used."

I agreed with her and did not say much after that. I heard the cassette compartment open and close. I knew musical sound would emanate from the speakers once the play button was depressed. I held my breath, as I wondered about her preferred musical genre. Pure, unadulterated country music came on. She sang along as Donna Fargo confessed that she was "the happiest girl in the whole USA." The song was thereafter etched in my memory because of the significance of the moment. She was a country western music lover and unapologetic about it. "Joseph, do you like country music?"

I fancied myself a refined gent and was more inclined to classical music. I did not want to offend her, so I said, "Francesca, I like some country music, and what you are playing sounds very good." She turned the volume up because of my approval of her choice of song.

It did not take long before the aroma of her cooking took over my imagination. I was not sure what she was cooking, since I could not see, but it smelled good. I was concerned about making a fool of myself, because I had to eat while blind. My mind wondered on what to do; feel my food with my fingers or just rely on trial and error with a fork?

When the cooking was done, she served my meal in the living room and giggled as she fed me. "Joseph, I am obligated to feed you, since I do not want you to hurt yourself with a knife." I protested initially about being fed, but gave in when she insisted. I was not visually stimulated before I took my first bite, but my palate gave her an A + in cooking. She'd made a southern fried steak with all the fixings; sautéed mushrooms, green pepper, red onions, and chopped celery. Her sweet potatoes were delightful and left my mouth watering for more. She dabbed my lips occasionally to remove excess sauce.

"Francesca, this is the best meal I have had since I left home."

She dabbed my lips again and said, "Thank you for the compliment."

Although I enjoyed and appreciated what Francesca did for me, I was worried that things were moving too fast between us. I could not share my concern with her because it would sound as if I did not appreciate what she was doing for me. I was still worrying about minor issues when Francesca complicated things more for me.

"I am spending the night here to make sure that you are cared for properly," she said after we finished our meals.

My heart was beating so fast that I could hear the pounding inside my chest. My lips quivered as I tried to speak.

Sensing that I was in agony over her proposal, she apologized for being too forward. "Joseph, I did not mean to take liberties, but I want to be here for you."

I searched for the right thing to say to her, but found none. Finally, I said something that sounded stupid. "You are not obligated to me, Francesca." It was evident to even a blind man that she took offense to my callousness. "I am indebted to you, Francesca. You did more than I would ever expect a friend to do for me."

I was about to say more when she kissed me. "I love you, Joseph. I have loved you since the first day we met."

I wondered how she could love me, since she hardly knew me. I knew love was a serious matter which I was not ready for at that time. All the responsibilities associated with it scared me. "Francesca, I do not deserve all you have done for me since we met, not to talk about loving me." I told her that I had nothing to offer a beautiful lady like herself who deserved more than I could ever give to her.

I was going on with a list of things I could not afford do for her when she stopped me again with a kiss. "I want us to be together, Joseph. I want to see you every day and do things with you. I feel special being with you."

She was so emotional with her request that I held her very tight. "Francesca, I am the one who feels special being with you," I protested. The gentleness of her voice and the softness of her touch were confirmation of true love, I thought.

"Joseph, you can't see Wendy any more. We have an exclusive relationship now."

It terrified me that Francesca was making rules for me and wanted to keep me away from the only friend I knew before her.

"Dance with me, Joseph. It will be our first dance." She walked to the dining table and replaced the cassette tape. She walked back and danced with me. I could not see, so I settled for what I imagined us to look like waltzing the night away.

# # #

Francesca probably wanted to be needed, and the opportunity presented itself. I felt responsible for my predicament.

If I'd been more careful in the chemistry laboratory and avoided my injury, we could have been in the library studying instead of testing the limits of our friendship. I was happy to be close to Francesca, but I was worried that a love affair would be financially difficult for me to sustain. I imagined all the things she probably loved to do that I could not afford. Due to my limited financial preparedness, I felt inadequate. I also felt that she pushed her agenda aggressively because of my physical vulnerability. While she relished our exclusive relationship, I was ambivalent about its viability. However, my negative feelings were not communicated to her.

I was excited to wake up on Saturday morning. It meant regaining my vision and independence. I wanted to go back to my old life without a girlfriend to tie me down. I was not sure what else Francesca would demand from me. I took my eye patches off in front of the mirror. My eyes were less irritated, and my vision was good. I rushed to the living room excited, but Francesca appeared unhappy. "Joseph, I want to spend more time with you this weekend. Hopefully, regaining your vision will not adversely affect our relationship. I hope you will continue to need me."

Her disappointment surprised me. "I will always be grateful to you, Francesca. I would have been lost without you," I said to her.

She smiled and hugged me. I suggested breakfast at the school cafeteria before morning studies at the main school library.

Chapter 11

It was difficult getting back to my daily routine with Francesca tagging along. Francesca needed more attention than I expected. She expected me to hold her hand all the time. Our open expression of affection became so frequent that I teased her about my lips requesting a 15-minute rest from hers. She apparently did not find my comment funny and wanted to know if I was tired of being with her. Things were moving so fast that I became worried about not being able to keep up with her.

I was very uncomfortable with the probing eyes of fellow students, too. The more we were observed and criticized, the more daring she became. One evening while I was studying alone in the library, Francesca stopped by to see me. At least eight students sat close by my desk, watching and listening to us. Their presence did not deter her from straddling me and mauling my lips. I was embarrassed but could not say much. "Joseph, you are mine and I want everyone to know it," she said.

I was a very private person who lost his anonymity because of unnecessary fanfare. Our cross-cultural relationship was not openly accepted, even on college campuses at that time. We were therefore exposed to hurtful comments from fellow students. "Go back to your jungle and hold hands with monkeys," one burly student said to me while his friends were cheering him on. Most of the comments were from male students who occasionally threatened me with physical harm.

I avoided direct confrontation with any student, but I defended myself when Francesca's sorority sister Verona called me an opportunistic ape. It was the first time I met Verona, who was their sorority local chapter president. She heard that I was dating Francesca and wanted to put an end to it. Her mission, as she said, was to protect their sorority reputation. So what she said to me was not a surprise. "Joseph, or whatever you are called, you're ruining my friend's future. Why can't you find your own kind and leave Francesca alone?"

Apparently she expected a response from me, but I ignored her. She became bolder with her verbal attack. "Francesca is going through a rebellious phase with you, ape man. I am sure that she will come back to her senses," Verona said to me.

I tried not to be perturbed by her comments, but could not keep silent any longer. "I demand an apology from you, Verona. Otherwise, I may report you to the school authorities for harassment."

While walking away from me she said, "Leave my sorority sister alone, you jungle bunny."

I sarcastically said to Verona, "Nice meeting you, too." As much as I tried to forget all the hurtful words Verona dumped on me, I could not stop the pain I felt inside me.

My life began to change for the better when I met with the chairman of my department two weeks after the school year started. I arrived at his office 15 minutes before my appointment. I was not sure why he needed to see me. I had made As in all the quizzes we had so far. Academically, I was the best student they had at that time.

When Dr. Ezir walked in, I politely stood up to greet him. He walked with a limp and complained about his hip pain. He told me that he was planning to retire in a few months as the chairman of the department but would remain as a faculty member. I was very concerned about his retirement until I heard him say, "Joseph, we are awarding you a departmental scholarship, based on your academic performance, and a small monthly stipend for research assistantship starting this semester. It is renewable every year, depending on the availability of funds and your academic performance."

Dr. Ezir had not finished what he was saying before tears of joy came over me. I felt that his proclamation validated my worthiness in a school where I faced discrimination by fellow students.

"Son, do not ever forget that you are here to learn and make something of yourself. You are a hard working student, and I am very proud of you." When he was done with his speech, he gave me an envelope that contained details of the awards. He also gave me an envelope to present to the bursar's office so that my student account would be credited. We shook hands before I left. It turned out to be a good day for me, after the verbal imbecility from Verona earlier that day.

I was overwhelmed by the financial support I received from the chemistry department, and I wanted very badly to share it with someone. I felt the need to write to Gina about my good news but needed Wendy's congratulatory hug. In my quest to reach out to my special friends who were more academically inclined, I forgot the appropriate pecking order that was in place. Francesca should have been the first person to know about my good news. Instead, I ran to Wendy's residence hall to tell her.

Wendy listened to my story and then asked, "Have you told Francesca about your awards?"

I did not hesitate to tell her that she was the first person I shared my good news with. "Find your girlfriend and tell her the good news," Wendy said. "I will pretend that you did not tell me about your scholarship when I see her. She should be the first to be told." I thanked her for looking out for me. "By the way, Joseph, I am happy for you and Francesca, but I miss our friendship."

I reminded her that she was the one who was uncomfortable with our friendship because of peer pressure. The exchange between us became awkward, but it reaffirmed my belief that Wendy was a genuine friend.

# # #

Several things changed my life for the better when I was in undergraduate school, but none compared to the effect the academic scholarship had on me. I had started the academic year with the loss of the valuable friendship I had with Wendy. Unfortunately, I did not have enough time to sort my life out before Francesca came along. Francesca's emergence as my new confidant could have been a positive thing for me, but her sudden transformation into a "girlfriend" morphed into a socioeconomic burden. I was spending more money than I had budgeted in food, since we ate together most of the time. We frequented pastry and ice cream parlors around campus, which was a significant deviation from my lifestyle. Although she offered to pay some of the time, I felt it was my duty to pay for both of us.

After my initial fear and aversion to a relationship, I became fond of Francesca. She was a beautiful and vivacious person who brought happiness to everyone close to her. She brought joy and a sense of fulfillment to my lonely campus life. There was never a dull moment with her infectious energy.

# # #

I had waited in front of the biology department for Francesca. When she emerged from her class, at least three young men were following her. Her tight-fitting red dress hugged her small waist line and accentuated her perfect bust. No detailed description of Francesca's body could ever do her justice. It had to be seen to be adequately appreciated. Simply put, she was a work of art.

Apart from her beauty, her sweet voice, with her unique intonations, could soften the most hardened soul.

"Oh! Joseph, have you been waiting for me long?" she said as soon as she saw me. Francesca's seductive sweet voice brought a smile to my face. "I know you missed me honey," she continued. She hugged me so hard that I had to plead with her to let me breathe. Her admirers dispersed when she focused her attention on me. They shook their heads in disbelief as they walked away. I quickly told her the details of my scholarship and my determination to become a better student.

"My love, Joseph, you are an excellent student already. We have to celebrate your good news first before you go back to bury your face in your books. Make time once in a while to look at my green eyes, and kiss my lips."

It was a very seductive proposal delivered to me with batting eyelashes. I was filled with immeasurable joy and a sense of fulfillment. I watched as Francesca's eyes glistened in the sun, and her face became more radiant.

"Joseph, why are you looking at me so intensely?" she said to me.

I did not have to search for an answer. "I am so happy to be with you, Francesca."

She was surprised by my candidness and shed tears of joy as she spoke. "Shucks Joseph, you know how to make a girl feel special."

I held her hand as we walked away from the classroom building. As always, we attracted so much attention from students walking to their classes.

My idea of celebration was an ice cream treat at the student center, but my mischievous friend had other plans. We were walking on a path toward the student center when she informed me about her own plan.

"We are going out to a disco club for celebration." She suggested a club that was popular with college students. Since I had never been to a disco club, I accepted her suggestion without further discussion. I only disagreed with the urgency of such celebration. I had imagined a weekend outing with our friends, but Francesca wanted an immediate celebration by the two of us.

We were very close to the ice cream vending area when she declined my offer of a light snack. She wanted to change her dress, so she opted to go back to her house. "I am too sexy in this outfit, and I don't want to cause any problems for these young boys on campus." She was partly joking and partly serious with her statement. I complimented her dress and agreed with her decision to change.

As soon we arrived at her place of residence, Francesca opened all the mails left on her bed. She became quiet and somber after she opened an envelope from the financial aid office of our school. I was alarmed at the sudden change in her demeanor. She became distant and withdrawn from me. I was afraid that the university authorities had dismissed her from school because of me. I knew my thoughts were irrational, but it was plausible, considering the state of social affairs at that time. I was relieved when she told me that she had no money to continue for the semester.

When Francesca registered for classes, it was conditional on approval of her financial aid request. Unfortunately, she had used all the available funds she was qualified to get in four years. She was a fifth year student in her final year, and apparently she had no other financial aid options from the university as an undergraduate student. Although tuition for in-state students was cheap in the mid-1970s, she could not afford to pay her way. Her mother, who was divorced from her father, could not afford to help her from her limited income as a nurse's aide. Her father stopped all financial support when she turned 18. She was in a dire situation and needed a quick solution.

Francesca listed all of her relatives that she could remember, but she could not come up with even a single one who could help her financially. She needed only two semesters of tuition to finish her bachelor's degree in biology. I was very concerned for her and was willing to help out any way I could. I quickly reviewed my own financial state silently. I had saved $500 during the summer vacation and was entitled to a partial refund from the university, since my tuition would be covered by my department scholarship. I felt that I had enough funds to help her with her in-state tuition.

"Francesca, how much is your tuition for the year?" I asked. I was so relieved when she told me that she had to pay $450 for the year as an in-state student. "I can loan you the money to pay your tuition." She probably did not hear what I said initially. "Francesca, I said that I could loan you the tuition money."

She held on to me while jumping up and down. I worked out the rest of our semester survival plan. Her monthly rent was minimal, since she was only renting a room. What was left was money for meals and basic needs. I worked out a system for us to conserve our daily expenditures. I had the meal plan that Wendy bequeathed to me that I could share with Francesca. We agreed on cooking dinner at my place to defray the cost of feeding the two of us.

"Joseph, as soon as I graduate in May, I will get a job and pay you back. I will never forget your kindness to me as long as I live. I will always be yours as long as you want me."

Chapter 12

I wandered onto a soccer field one Saturday morning while waiting for the library to open. I was surprised to see many students playing soccer that early in the morning. Most of the players were foreign students from Iran, Ethiopia, South America, and India. I spoke to a student that I felt was the coordinator of the game. Jala, who was from Iran, told me that I was welcome to join them any Saturday morning I had time. He introduced me to the rest of the players.

"Thank you, Jala. I plan to play with you guys next weekend." I watched their game for a few minutes before I went back to the library.

I informed Francesca about my plan to play soccer early on Saturdays. This was also a way to get needed exercise, and I felt that it would break the monotony of studying all the time. Although she did not know much about soccer, she was excited that I had other interests apart from studying. She promised to come to the field to watch me play. "Joseph, I plan to come with my pom-poms to cheer you on Saturday," Francesca teased me.

It was a very nice fall Saturday morning when I arrived at the soccer field. The day was dry and less humid than usual. Jala was the only one on the soccer field when I arrived. He introduced himself again to me. "I am an engineering student from Iran. I live with my sister Marian, who is also an engineering student. My father is a minister under the Shah of Iran," Jala proudly told me. He went on to tell me more about his family. When he enrolled in school with his sister, their mother came with them, apparently to help them with domestic issues. Instead of living in a school dormitory, their father bought a three-bedroom house for them.

Jala had to stop telling me about himself when the other players arrived. We were about to start playing when Francesca arrived to watch me. She wore a pair of white shorts and a red top. Her red tennis shoes complemented her outfit, but they also stood out. She gregariously approached the soccer field, attracting the attention of the soccer players. Predictably, some of the boys whistled as she got closer to me. She appeared unperturbed as she ran to hug and kiss me.

I introduced Francesca to the soccer players. She shook everyone's hand and teased them about their ungentlemanly behavior toward a lady. She emphasized the word lady as she spoke to them. She had a hearty exchange with some of the players and declined the offer to play with us.

When the game was over, I had an intense discussion with Jala after all the other players were gone. He was a very carefree, friendly young man with progressive ideas. It was, therefore, not surprising to me that he was interested in my unique relationship with Francesca. He wondered how we handled all the scrutiny and verbal abuse we were exposed to in a small university town.

"Jala, I am not worried about what people think of me. I am here to get an education. That is what I concentrate on. They may not like me, but I try to make them respect me. I try to be the best student that I can be."

He could sense that I was angry with the system by the tone of my voice. "Joseph, I understand how you feel. I am very open-minded and hope that we remain friends. Please ignore all the narrow minded bigots on campus." Jala's words were very supportive.

Before we left, he invited us to dinner with his family. Francesca and I accepted his invitation without hesitation. "Joseph, my mother cooks well, and I am sure you will enjoy Persian cuisine," Jala said to me after I accepted his invitation. We agreed on showing up for dinner at six that evening. After exchanging addresses and telephone numbers with Jala, I headed for the men's locker room in the gymnasium. Francesca followed me up to the door of the locker room and sat down. I quickly showered, then put on a clean pair of pants and a cotton shirt.

When I came out of the locker room, Francesca looked me over and apparently was not happy with my choice of clothes. She refused to tell me what was wrong with what I had on. She only said, "You are a smart man, Joseph. Figure it out."

I begged her to tell me what was wrong with my outfit several times. She finally gave in to my request. "I had expected you to wear something red for me, Joseph. Don't you love me? You are supposed to do things that make me happy."

I looked at Francesca and playfully told her that I was sorry for letting her down. She made faces at me, then puckered her lips. I looked away as if I did not see her last facial expression. She grabbed my right arm, spun me around, and playfully bit my neck. She chased me as I ran away from her. We acted like children in a playground. She was very fond of carefree times like that.

# # #

For the dinner invitation, I asked Francesca to dress conservatively. She was unhappy with my suggestion, so we debated on the pitfalls of intercultural socialization. She did not know much about Persian culture and had no interest in what was considered appropriate clothing for a dinner invitation. She eventually saw things my way and settled for a beautiful black dress that was culture neutral.

"Joseph, I compromise a lot for you. I always dress to please you. What is wrong with me showing my beautiful legs?" Although Francesca was teasing me with her statement, I knew she felt frustrated with the formality of an evening dinner with a friend's family.

Jala had offered to pick us up from my apartment, but Francesca insisted on driving. She picked me up 25 minutes before we were expected to arrive for our dinner invitation. I took some time to look her over. She looked dazzling in her black dress. Every curve on her body was accentuated, and her narrow waistline was hugged by a wide silver belt. Her hair smelled like fresh flowers, and her green eyes looked more seductive than ever. "You look ravishing Francesca," I said.

"Joseph, we can skip the dinner if that is what you have in mind."

I teased her for always trying to seduce me. We left my apartment before we could give in to physical temptation. I sat quietly on the passenger side, watching Francesca drive. She was serious for the first time since we'd met. She was a very good driver and was concerned about our safety. We arrived at our destination on time.

We were let into the house by Marian. Their house was tastefully decorated. The living room and family rooms were decorated with French antique furniture. We were shown around the house with a full explanation of the importance of various pieces of furniture. According to Marian, they chose their rugs first before they bought the furniture to go with them.

Their mother was a middle-aged beautiful lady who was raised in France but moved to Iran after she got married. She spoke fluent French and was amused by my failed attempts to converse with her in my high school level French grammar. "Monsieur Joseph, I do understand English. May we converse in English instead of French? I want to improve on my English," she said.

Francesca, who did not say much initially, agreed with the suggestion of English as the language of choice for the evening. Marian led the way to their dining room, where every popular Persian dish was ready to be served. We were advised to sample everything rather than have a full serving of only one dish. I was so overwhelmed by the amount of food that I did not know where to start.

As we sat down to eat, Marian played a French song on their grand piano. She was a very talented pianist. Her mother vocalized the song as she played. We gathered around the piano to listen to Marian and her mother. I felt as if we were old friends who came by to visit.

"Let us eat before the food gets cold," Jala said. He probably was hungry and had no interest in the music. We went back to the dining room.

As our conversation progressed during dinner, it became clear that Jala had an ulterior motive when he invited us for dinner. His parents were against cross-ethnic dating and marriage. He probably felt that I had an exemplary relationship with Francesca which could be used to convince his mother that intercultural relationships worked out for some people.

"Mother, do you see how Joseph and Francesca get along?" Jala was serious when he spoke to his mother.

His mother ignored his question until Marian made a comment. "Mother, ignoring reality does not invalidate the truth."

Their mother looked at Marian with a facial expression that spoke of betrayal. She continued with her silence, stood up, and excused herself from the dining room.

When she returned 15 minutes later, it was obvious that she had cried. Marian told us that her mother's parents had refused to let her marry an Egyptian she met in school. They were against mixed marriages and felt that children of such unions would grow up with confused identities.

"Joseph, how long have you known Francesca?"

I had to look at the matriarch of the family twice when she asked me that question. I hesitated before I answered her question, since my answer could have a great impact on my new friends. "I have known Francesca for more than one year, but we became close friends recently."

I was not done with my answer when Francesca corrected me. "Joseph, we are lovers, not friends. Am I just a friend to you, Joseph?" Francesca sounded very disappointed with me.

"Francesca, I meant very special friends."

Our hostess appeared amused by our bickering. Francesca leaned over and kissed me. "As you can see, we are lovers and not friends. Joseph, friends don't kiss the way we do." The dining room erupted with laughter.

I tried to change the conversation, but more questions were asked that brought us back to intercultural dating and marriage. "Joseph, are you planning to marry Francesca?" It was a profound question from Marian.

"Marian, we are still in school and have not thought about marriage. We are still getting to know each other." I had to explain to her what marriage meant to me. I told her that I was a traditionalist who believed that a man was responsible for his family financially. However, I agreed that marriage was a joint partnership with equal rights for each partner.

"What is the most important thing in a marriage?" Marian asked.

I was about to answer her question when Francesca answered first. "I believe that the most important thing about marriage is love."

Marian turned to Francesca and asked, "Do you love Joseph?"

Francesca stood up, walked over to me, and pulled me up from my chair. "Marian, let us change things around. Joseph is the one to answer your question, not me." Francesca held me around the waist and asked, "Joseph, do you love me.?"

It was the highest drama of the night. Francesca used an opportunity Marian created to find out if I was in love with her. It felt like an eternity before I answered her question. I could not find a direct answer to her question. I held Francesca tighter as a way to express my feelings towards her but could not answer verbally. It was an awkward moment for the two of us. I finally answered her question without direct commitment. "Francesca, if you are still in doubt about my feelings toward you, I believe that we have a problem," I said to her.

Francesca did not accept my answer. "Joseph, it is very simple. Do you love me?" She was very emphatic with her question.

"Of course I do, Francesca," I retorted.

The matriarch of the house watched with great interest as I struggled with a simple question. She did not hesitate to use my fallible answer to emphasize the point she made to her children about the importance of intra-cultural marriage. "Where do you plan to live after you get married?"

Her children watched in disbelief as she tried to expose my lack of commitment to a simple relationship. I explained to her that I was not ready to get married to anyone at that time. "In my country, Iran, love means marriage," she scolded me.

As their mother continued to scold me, it was obvious that she was winning the battle of wits her children started. They switched to the Persian language and asked their mother to stop asking me too many questions.

As soon as the embarrassing questions stopped, I used the opportunity to announce our intention to leave. "I am very grateful for your hospitality and a lively discussion," I said.

As I stood up to leave, their mother said, "Joseph and Francesca, this is your home, too. Come to visit any time."

Jala and Marian repeated what their mother said about an open invitation to their house any time we wanted to visit.

When we got in the car, Francesca did not speak to me. It was evident that I'd disappointed her. I did not try to defend myself because it could make things worse. When we reached my apartment, I asked her to spend the night since it was late, but she declined my offer and left without saying goodbye.

I was changing my clothes when I heard a knock on my door. "Joseph, open the door. I can't stay mad at you long."

I was happy that she came back, since we had a lot to talk about. "I am happy that you came back. I am very sorry if I offended you tonight."

She entered my apartment and walked to the bathroom. It was obvious that she had been crying. When she emerged from the bathroom, we sat on the davenport looking at each with unflappable determination. It was obvious that things were not right between us. "Francesca, I am not sure what you really want from me. I care about you, but it seems that you want more than I can give you at this time. I do not know what is left for me to do."

She appeared restless but tried to control herself. "Joseph, why is it difficult for you to say that you love me?" she yelled.

I explained to her that our discussion tonight centered on love with commitment to marriage and not on a love affair between two college students. "We are still in school and do not have the resources to nurture a long-term commitment. I am a foreign student trying to understand your lifestyle, and you have not even begun to understand my background or culture."

I was not even done when Francesca yelled at me again. "You always have excuses about everything, Saint Joseph.

You are afraid to touch me. You always talk about doing the right thing. If you love me, go ahead and show me."

I was uncomfortable with her outburst. "I did not know that things were that bad between us, Francesca. I am very sorry if I made you miserable." I was moved by her anguish. I felt that she was vulnerable since she had limited financial resources. I did not want her to feel that she was obligated to me because I loaned her money for her tuition. I tried to explain why I was distant, but she did not accept my excuses. "I promise to be more attentive to you, Francesca. I will never take you for granted."

She smiled for the first time since we'd left our Iranian friends. "I don't want to lose you, Joseph. I love you more every day, and I want to be yours."

My hands trembled, and my lips quivered as she confessed her love for me. Cold sweat drenched my face as Francesca continued with her pledge of an exclusive love affair between us. "I love you too, Francesca, but we should not let anything distract us from our school work."

I was afraid of getting emotionally dependent on Francesca. We did not have much in common, and I could not imagine spending the rest of my life with her. She felt the opposite about me and tried her best to show that she cared about me.

After we talked all night about our friendship, things improved between us. It was evident in so many ways that she was happy again with me. She playfully imitated my accent, tried to walk with my big shoes, and loved it when I chased her around. She knew how to initiate a chase and perfected how to fall on the grass while running. Francesca made me appreciate things I took for granted, as we broke all the unwritten social rules at that time in central North Carolina. Our picnics never ended with sunsets as expected, since we imagined the sun to be shining when darkness took over us. Our times together were carefree and memorable. She became the sunshine I needed to wake up in the morning and the moonlight that made my dreams more meaningful.

As Francesca finally put it to me, "Joseph, we are in love with each other."

Chapter 13

I heard from Gina a few days before Thanksgiving. We had spoken on the telephone a few days before her postcard arrived. She had gone to Walt Disney World with some friends and felt obligated to send me a note. She had been very busy since she started medical school.

Joseph,

Surely you're surprised to hear from me so soon. This is my way of expressing how great it was to hear your voice and to know that you were thinking of me. The friendship we share is beautiful and you will forever be a very special man in my life.

I will be home for Thanksgiving and I hope that you will spend the holiday with my family. Please do not make any other plans.

Love always,

Your sister Gina.

I shared Gina's postcard with Francesca, who felt threatened because I would spend the Thanksgiving holiday without her. She had planned to spend time with her mother and brother before I showed her the postcard. "I am happy that you are going home to spend some time with your family. I will be here waiting for you when you come back," I said to Francesca as she held the postcard from Gina with contempt. I could sense that she was ambivalent about going home. It was difficult to say if she was worried about my welfare and loneliness or was jealous of my closeness with Gina. Whatever she felt was not disclosed to me.

Two days before Thanksgiving day, Francesca left for a one-week vacation with her family. We were with Gina before Francesca left. We had gone to Gina's house to welcome her back from school. I felt that Francesca needed reassurance that Gina was not someone I was enamored with.

The reunion was memorable for me because it was obvious that Gina missed me. Gina held on to me for at least ten minutes before she said anything to Francesca. "I missed you, Joseph," Gina said to me. She looked me over and said, "Joseph, you have lost a lot of weight. I asked you to visit my house often for dinner, but you did not. My Mom was ready to feed you, but you never visited."

I waited until she was done with her scolding before I spoke. "Gina, this is Francesca, my girlfriend I spoke to you about." Francesca was surprised that I introduced her as my girlfriend. I felt the need to use all the words that would make Francesca comfortable with Gina.

"Francesca, have we not met before?" Gina was very sure that they knew each other but could not remember how and where they met. "Thank you, Francesca, for taking care of my brother Joseph. I will look after him while you are gone."

It was obvious that Francesca did not like Gina's possessiveness. It was only after we left Gina's house that she complained to me. "Your fake sister is full of herself, Joseph." I smiled without making any comment.

# # #

Francesca left me with a cloudy Carolina sky and desolateness. I could not weep, but the clouds wept for me. It was a torrential rainfall that left me helpless. My state of hopelessness made me realize how much I needed Francesca. She had become a part of me. I stayed home during Thanksgiving recess, catching up with letters to my parents and siblings. I turned down the invitation for Thanksgiving dinner with Gina. I preferred time alone for reflection. When and how I became so attached to Francesca was hard for me to decipher. I felt vulnerable and was afraid that it was too late for me to change things. I wondered what I could do to reverse things. I wondered out loud,. "Is Francesca feeling the same without me?" I had no answer to my question. I fell asleep on my davenport pondering what to do.

One week felt like a lifetime, but Francesca eventually came back to school. She apparently enjoyed her visit home. She spent some time with her mother and grandparents. It was obvious that she missed me. She came back in the morning and drove to my apartment first. In her typical exaggerated southern drawl, she summed everything in one incomplete sentence. "I had missed you so." I took it to mean that she missed me a lot. Our hug lasted for a long time. The kiss was more of slobber than a refined lip interlock. We spent the morning talking about her experience at home and her mother's desire to meet me. Her grandparents apparently wanted to meet me, too. Her grandfather was in North Africa and France during the Second World War. He considered himself well travelled and would love the opportunity to meet with a foreigner who might have been to the places he passed through as a soldier.

I had breakfast with Francesca before we drove to her place. I helped her unload her winter clothes that she brought from home. She took all her summer clothes home during the Thanksgiving break, since the fall weather was colder than expected. She had an impressive collection of coats, pants, and tops. I was amazed at her wardrobe. She had more clothes than an average college student. She even had real fur coats. According to Francesca, she spent all her summer earned income buying clothes. Appearance apparently meant everything to her.

When we were done hanging her clothes, we went to the kitchen to get something to drink. Before she opened the refrigerator she said, "Joseph, I am invited to New York City by a modeling agency to compete for the front cover of the June edition of a sports magazine. They are looking for amateur college student models for this year's special edition of the magazine. I have to travel to New York City next week. Joseph, I am so excited."

I was surprised that she had an interest in professional modeling. "How about your class work, and physics in particular, which you need to graduate in May?"

She smiled before she answered my question. "I will be gone for only three days. They sent all the information to my mother's house. I wish you could go with me."

I had no interest in going to New York City with Francesca. I gave my education priority and turned down her offer. I did not ask where she would get the money to pay my way to New York City. I guess with the excitement of being invited for a modeling job, she forgot that I used my savings to pay her tuition for the semester. Her next semester's tuition and fees were also due in one month. It was therefore necessary to conserve all the funds I had. Apparently, school was the last thing on her mind that day.

When classes started on Monday after the Thanksgiving break, I asked Francesca to meet with all her professors to review her academic progress and get permission before she travelled to New York City. She did not argue with me. "Joseph, you are so smart. You think about everything. Little old me thought about my trip and nothing else. I love you, Joseph."

I emphasized to her the need for us to spend more time in the library, since she appeared distracted from her studies. "I will do anything for you, my love," she said to me.

I had to correct her. "Francesca, you are studying for you, and not for me. You have to study to graduate in May." She jokingly told me that I was worried about my money going to waste.

Seven days went by fast. We spent every available time studying together. We covered some of the topics in physics that she would miss. I felt that she grasped the concepts, and I was confident that she would do well if we were tested in the areas we covered. On Sunday night after we had dinner, she left for New York City. It was her first flight. Instead of feeling anxious, she appeared excited. "I am so happy that I will fly to New York City rather than take a bus. I will buy souvenirs for you, my love."

I told her to save the $50 I gave her for emergencies. The modeling agencies paid for the trip, but she needed some money for incidentals. She was very grateful about the financial assistance I rendered to her.

# # #

We had waited for her departure at the terminal gate. She sat on my lap as we waited. The departure terminal was packed with passengers and family members. A young child walked up to Francesca and asked, "Why are you sitting on his lap? Is he your daddy?" He was barely three years old and apparently was amused at the public display of affection between us. His mother apologized and took her son away.

Ethnically mixed couples were rare in central North Carolina in those years, but what was never seen was such couple engaged in public displays of affection. Whispered discontentment pervaded our surroundings, but Francesca was not deterred. She kissed and caressed my neck with total disregard for other waiting passengers. I pleaded with her to show some restraint, but she ignored my request. "Joseph, this is a free country, and we are not committing any crime."

An older lady sitting next to us heard what Francesca said and was very angry. She addressed Francesca with a stern voice. "Young lady, if your pantie is on fire, go somewhere private and put it out."

Francesca ignored her comment but stopped caressing my neck. She was the embodiment of a provocative coed.

Time went faster than I expected, as if someone manually moved it forward when I was distracted by Francesca. I was relieved when all the probing eyes moved away from the two of us to the boarding gate. No tears were shed, because Francesca was excited about her first flight. We hugged briefly before she ran toward the gate to be checked in.

"Bye, Joseph. I am going to miss you."

"Bye Francesca. Be careful in New York City."

I felt empty going back home alone. Francesca's perfume clung to me after our last embrace. She probably left her scent on me on purpose with noble thoughts, but it made her absence more unbearable for me. I smiled when I remembered her famous line. "I am always with you, Joseph." For two days while she was gone, her perfume stuck to my shirt like our first sensuous embrace. I had now reached a stage where I needed Francesca emotionally. It was a worrying sign for me.

Chapter 14

On a very cold fall day, Francesca took me to meet her mother and grandparents. They lived 60 miles away from our college town. I was very anxious about meeting her family. She had requested a weekend visit, but her mother approved only a Saturday afternoon get together. We were to meet her grandparents first for lunch, before visiting her mother. We arrived at her grandparents' house a few minutes before noon. Her grandmother opened the front door to welcome us. She was in her early 70s, slightly overweight, and had curly gray hair. Although it was late fall and cold, she had a summer dress on. She smiled as we entered the partition between their family room and dining room.

Francesca was on her best behavior and was not holding my hand as usual. "Grandma, you look as beautiful as ever." Her grandmother smiled and hugged her. "This is my friend Joseph from school. Grandma, he has been away from his home for a long time, and I have been taking care of him at school."

Her grandmother, Ethel, shook my hand without saying much. It was hard for me to discern what her silence meant. I walked behind Francesca into the family room, which was decorated with mismatched furniture. The room was poorly lit with old dingy lamps. There was no theme to their decoration. It appeared that any available piece of furniture was placed where there was space. The walls were darkly painted, and old photographs were hung on them without proper leveling. The aroma of baked pie pervaded the air inside the room. Apparently there was no desire to air out the house before we arrived.

"Grandma, are you baking your famous pecan pie?" Francesca appeared more interested in what was baking in the kitchen. Her grandfather walked into the family room while smoking a pipe. He shook my hand first before he hugged his granddaughter. He looked younger than his age, and he was wearing a pair of blue jean overalls. His skin was tanned to the texture of leather from overexposure to the sun.

"Grandpa, are you still smoking tobacco from your farm?" Francesca inquired.

He emptied his pipe before he answered her. "I grow the best tobacco in the county, and I still sample the best tobacco this side of the Mississippi." He cleared his throat before he continued. He turned toward me and asked, "Do you smoke, son?"

I did not hesitate to answer him. "No sir, I do not smoke."

He looked at me quizzically and asked if I liked home-made whiskey. "No sir, I don't drink."

He laughed sardonically and cleared his throat again. "You don't smoke, and you don't drink. What the heck do you do?"

I smiled mischievously before I answered his question. "Sir, I am a student and a Christian." He appeared offended by my reply. "I did not mean to be disrespectful, but I have no need for alcohol and tobacco. My parents told me that they were bad habits that I should avoid."

He walked away from me and went outside to bring in firewood for his fireplace. I felt that I made a bad first impression. When he returned with his firewood, he smiled at me before he sat down. "You are right son; tobacco and alcohol are not good for you. Sit next to me and tell me about your country."

We had a long discussion about my country and his experiences during the Second World War. Unfortunately, our conversation was prematurely interrupted by his wife, who requested our presence in their dining room.

I was surprised that Francesca avoided sitting next to me. She sat next to her grandmother and hardly spoke to me. She acted as if we were not close. I was even more surprised when her grandfather prayed before we had our meal. "Bow your heads for a prayer. Dear Lord, we are gathered here for a meal that you provided for us. Let this meal nourish our body and soul. We give you thanks for your love and blessings. I am happy, dear Lord, that my granddaughter is here with us today. Please help her find a suitable man to marry."

I did not need to be told that I was not a suitable man for their granddaughter. I paid no further attention to the rest of his prayer after the plea for a worthy suitor. When I heard "Amen" from them, I knew the prayer was over. I managed to fake a smile and politely thanked them for inviting me to their dinner table.

We were served country style fried beef steak, corn bread, string beans, mashed potatoes, and pecan pie for desert. I used my cutlery in a formal fashion; knife held with the right hand and my fork with the left hand.

The silence that followed his prayer was unbearable, so I had to speak. "Francesca, your grandmother is a good cook." I spoke to her to draw her attention toward me. She had not spoken to me since we arrived at the house. She smiled at me without saying anything. Her silence spoke volumes of her uneasiness around her grandparents. Did she believe as they did, that I was not the right person for her? I could not answer that question, since she avoided any interaction with me.

"How did you meet my granddaughter?" It was the first thing her grandmother said to me.

"We met in our physics class, and we have been close friends since."

I was telling her details of our life together on campus when Francesca interrupted me. "Joseph, they are not interested in all that." I realized that she did not want them to know about our relationship.

"Your granddaughter has been nice to me, and she helped me out in school when I injured my eyes." The story I told sounded as if I was helpless and Francesca rescued me. I saw them smile as they spoke in unison, "That is our Francesca."

Francesca sat through the discussion without saying much. It was unnerving for me; to be taken to meet her grandparents without being properly introduced. I quickly changed to the person Francesca wanted me to be at that particular time; a good friend from school. I became just a casual school friend invited for lunch because of their granddaughter's generosity. That was the way it was presented, and that was the way the visit ended. I thanked them for their hospitality when I stood up to leave with Francesca and sauntered out, embarrassed. I did not look at Francesca until we arrived at her mother's house, which was less than a mile away.

I felt that she did not owe me an explanation, or an apology, for treating me like a stranger. However, when I could not stand the silence any more, I spoke up. "I am very sorry, Francesca, if I embarrassed you today in front of your grandparents."

She ignored me as tears flowed from her eyes. "Joseph, you would not understand. Things are different here as compared to a university, where we are free to be who we want to be. They would not understand nor accept our relationship. They are too old to change their views."

I felt her pain at that moment but did not know the right thing to say. "As I said before, Francesca, I am very sorry. Are you sure your mother wants to meet me?" She ignored my question.

Francesca's mother met us outside her door. She was dressed for work because she was called in to work for a sick coworker. She was different from what I expected. Francesca was very particular about what she wore and how she put on her makeup. Her mother was the opposite. She only had on lipstick, and her work clothes were not properly ironed. She probably did not care about what I thought of her appearance. She was beautiful, in spite of being overweight.

Her house was very small with slightly damaged aluminum siding. I could not help but thought of such a small place being washed away by a heavy rainfall. It did not fit the image Francesca portrayed in school. It was obvious that her mother was barely surviving financially. The only admirable thing about their situation was that Francesca was not ashamed of her family.

There was not much introduction necessary, because her mother was in a hurry to leave. She shook my hand while still walking. "Hello, Joseph, nice to meet you. I am sorry that I have to leave, but I will see you when I visit Francesca in school." She opened her car door before she spoke to Francesca. "Bye, Francesca." Her mother hurriedly left. Her old car left a plume of dark smoke behind. I deduced from the loud noise coming from her car that she had a malfunctioning exhaust pipe. I watched as her car was lost in the distance with dissipating black smoke.

I turned around to face Francesca, who was looking at me with anger and disapproval. She probably thought that I had a negative impression of her mother and their place of abode.

"Francesca, can we drive back to school? It has been a long day, and we need to study."

She sensed that I was tired and said, "I agree with you, Joseph, it has been a long day." It was a big relief for me, because I had no interest in seeing the inside of her house. I felt that some things are better left to one's imagination. I knew that the tension between us could be worse if my probing eyes were left to wander freely inside her house. It would not be fair to humiliate her further.

Chapter 15

A few days before the end of the fall semester, Wendy visited my apartment to drop off my Christmas present. She arrived ten minutes earlier than I expected. I had not seen her for more than one month. I was happy to see her, but I was also anxious. She had avoided me since Francesca became a part of my life. She probably felt that spending time with me would not be acceptable to her friend. I understood her mindset and did not complain.

Wendy was very special in so many ways, but some of her qualities stood out. She was a caring person that made me feel special. She had a remarkable gift of true friendship, and her presence brought joy, even when I was unhappy. She did not fail to lift me up emotionally on that day. With Wendy, I felt deep love and admiration that did not need to be expressed. Times I spent with her were like an emotional intermezzo that I did not need to consummate physically to feel fulfilled.

I had sweaty palms and a queasy stomach when I opened my front door to let Wendy inside. It was the highest level of anxiety I'd had in a long time.

"Hello, Joseph. It has been long for us." I held the door as Wendy walked in. She looked more beautiful than the last time I saw her. Although she always dressed fashionably, her appearance was more exquisite that morning. There was no overdone makeup or gaudy outfit for Wendy. She wore a simple long black skirt and a worsted wool red blazer. Her golden hair had grown longer since I last saw her, and it glistened in the early morning Carolina sun. Her long black leather boots complemented the coordinated red and black attire. She looked more like a business mogul than a college student. Her silver necklaces were missing from her neck, and in their place was a simple gold necklace.

We embraced as we used to do, and for a moment, time stood still for us. We were back to when we used to be the inseparable vanilla and cocoa. I kissed her cheeks again as we separated from a warm embrace. "So Joseph, you remembered to kiss my right cheek first before my left?"

I felt elated because she appreciated my friendly gesture. "How could I forget, Wendy? You had turned me into a cheek-kissing gentleman." She walked to the window in a pensive mood and gazed out for a few minutes. The sun illuminated her beautiful face more as she stood silent. I was reluctant to disrupt what was going through her mind. When she turned around to face me, her face was sad. We were silent for a long time as we stared at each other. No words were needed, because we felt connected to each other emotionally. We knew why we felt sad at that moment and did not have to express it.

When her smile resurfaced, I felt relieved. It was a painful emotional journey that led to nowhere. I was searching endlessly for the right thing to say but could not come up with the right words. Wendy finally spoke. "Joseph, I miss our friendship terribly." She waited for me to say something, but I did not. She continued with her speech. "We need to study together next semester. I spoke to Francesca about it, and she has no problems with us studying together." She walked back and forth as she spoke. She refused to sit down, because she was in a hurry to travel home, but she was not hurrying to leave. She avoided eye contact as she paced around.

Thirty minutes must have passed before Wendy finally gave me a wrapped present and asked me to open it after she left. I ignored her instructions and hurriedly tore through the paper wrapper like a child opening his first Christmas present. "Wendy, I love my first black leather coat, and a pair of gloves." I apologized for not buying her a Christmas present because I did not expect to see her before she left for the end-of-year break. Moreover, I did not know that she still thought about me. "I will make it up to you when we get back to school in January, Wendy."

I walked her to her car and opened and held the driver's door, but she stood there looking at me. Tears mixed with mascara rolled down her cheeks as she sobbed. We stood there as if we were saying a final goodbye to each other. She wiped her face before she looked at me. Our hands grasped with a surprise warmness that I felt was an emotional nonverbal reassurance of a unique commitment to each other. "I messed things up with you, Joseph." Wendy finally said.

I looked away briefly because my own tears were embarrassing me. I eventually leaned over and said to her, "You will always be a dear friend to me, Wendy." She hurriedly put on her sunshade to hide her tears and drove away.

It was a painful moment for me. Wendy ended our friendship because of the cross-cultural burden that she was not ready to shoulder. It was obvious that she cared for my wellbeing. However, I was entangled in a relationship with Francesca and could not go back to the Wendy and Joseph show, as I fondly labeled our friendship.

# # #

Francesca's departure for the Christmas vacation with her family was less dramatic. I was emotionally spent by the time I went over to her place. She was aware that Wendy had stopped by to see me. "How do you like your new leather coat? I helped Wendy pick the right size for you."

I was relieved that she was not jealous about my friendship with Wendy. "Make sure you send a thank you card to Wendy."

I nodded my head and loaded the rest of her things in the car. I was emotionally distant, but Francesca did not notice. She was excited about going home and was not very concerned about my state of mind. She left after her belongings were loaded in the car without much fanfare.

"See you in two weeks Joseph, and be good." No tears were shed, and our embrace was colder than a windy snowy morning. I felt lost in my own world as I walked back to my apartment.

Chapter 16

F rancesca returned to school the day before her classes started. She felt elated about coming back for the last semester of her last year. She was already in a festive mood before the semester even started. I felt that her state of mind could be beneficial as she transitioned to a self-assured woman. My only fear was the possible neglect of her academic responsibilities. We took the second physics class and microbiology together. It offered me the opportunity to monitor her progress. Although she left for her Christmas vacation unceremoniously, she returned to school with her characteristic public display of seductive affection.

We met at the student union building by her request for a snack. It was packed with returned students searching for their friends. As always, all eyes were on us as we walked to the dining area. Francesca held on to my waist as we walked in tandem. Our provocative entrance caused the familiar facial expression of disgust by some students and unsolicited negative comments by others. Francesca was not fazed by the negative reaction of some fellow students. She hung on to me as if we were glued together. There was no doubt in my mind that she felt comfortable with me and our relationship.

"Joseph, what is your pleasure today; me or the snack?" she joked, as we were standing for our turn to be served. Any answer I gave would have been wrong, so I smiled. It was typical of her to incite others to see my reaction.

A girl in front of her heard what she asked me, turned around, and admonished us with her hateful stare. She whispered to her friend, who also turned around to look at us. Their behavior was not different from what we had endured since we started spending time together. Most of the hate comments were directed at me. I was shocked when one of the girls addressed Francesca directly. "What are you doing with that loser? Look at him. He does not even look like us."

Francesca was angry but controlled herself. I begged her to remain calm. It was obvious that the girl wanted an open confrontation with us. It was the first time I was rattled by raw hatred directed at me by a female student. Her bold statement attracted other students, who wrongfully thought that I would spar with her. The large dining room felt small to me as other students approached to witness my reaction. The loud pounding of my heart drummed away the noise around me. I felt warm inside out of fear of a mob action. I quickly realized that the best thing to do was to ignore the girl. She taunted me with more hateful words, but my resolve was strong.

My next action surprised Francesca. I walked closer to the girl and spoke to her firmly. "I am very sorry if I offended you, but you have to get used to seeing the two of us together on this campus." I had a smirk on my face, which angered her more. She raised her hand to punch my face but was held back by her friend. Her companion probably felt embarrassed, and they walked away. If it were not for providence, things could have been worse. The crowd around us dispersed when they realized that she was the provocateur. We were served our snacks without further incidence.

We were almost done with our snacks when Wendy walked in. She sat next to Francesca but could not stop staring at me. I felt uncomfortable and avoided looking up for a long time. Their conversation was about Christmas shopping and the amount of food consumed during the holiday. I was in a partial hypnotic state when I heard Francesca call my name. My mind had wondered off to the last time I saw Wendy. I remembered her sorrow and uncontrollable wailing. I wondered how she could sit in front of me elated, as if she was happy for Francesca and me.

"Joseph, why are you ignoring Wendy's question?"

I was not aware that I was asked a question. "I am very sorry, Wendy, but I did not hear your question."

Wendy looked at me in disbelief. "Joseph, am I disturbing your lunch with Francesca? I am very sorry for inviting myself to your table."

I was puzzled by her false assumption. "I am very sorry, Wendy. Do you mind repeating your question?"

She looked at me and smiled. "It is too late now, Joseph. Francesca already answered my question." I could sense that she was not offended but was curious about my unusual disquiet.

"Wendy, we were verbally abused by some students while waiting to be served. That is why Joseph is acting very peculiar, I think." Since I felt that it was a better explanation for my behavior, I accepted Francesca's statement without argument.

Chapter 17

I believed that I had an honest relationship with Francesca and was therefore compelled to help her in any way that I could. We reviewed her financial obligation to the university before she completed her registration for her last semester. She owed partial tuition and graduation fees. She also had cap and gown costs added to her fees. She had no money to offset some of her college costs, and the financial burden became mine. I paid her remaining tuition and fees without hesitation.

"I will pay you back as soon as I graduate and start working." Her promise to repay me was good enough collateral. I felt that no contract was needed between friends.

I had only $50 left after I paid all her fees and had to depend on the monthly stipend from my department to survive. My stipend covered my monthly expenditures, with $75 remaining every month. I paid for Francesca's room, which was $25 monthly, with the money that was left from my stipend. We lived on the remaining $50 and Wendy's school meal plan.

"You are a life saver," Francesca said. She apparently felt relieved after all her outstanding fees were paid.

"Helping to pay your school fees is not the same as saving your life," I jokingly said. She nodded her head in agreement. I knew that such precarious financial vulnerability could be embarrassing to her, so I quickly changed our discussion to a more pleasant topic.

# # #

I was happy when classes started. It was an opportunity to focus on my studies with no time left to worry about personal issues. Since Wendy had asked to study with me, I knew that things would be different between us. Our study group that semester was made up of Francesca, Lisa, Wendy, Virgil, and me. Virgil was Lisa's new friend and a likable fellow. However, he had no study discipline. He was a basketball player who lost his starting position with the school team because of a failed class the previous semester.

He had to be taught how to concentrate during our study period and how to avoid inappropriate pranks. I explained my study rules to him. "Virgil, we do not talk or play footsie during the two hours of study block. We take a 15-minute break after two hours of uninterrupted study time. You can play with Lisa then." Everyone laughed while I was addressing Virgil.

I studied alone with Wendy early on Saturday mornings because she needed my help with applied mathematics. Early one Saturday morning, she mustered the courage to ask me a defining question. "Joseph, why do you like me?"

It was an unexpected question from Wendy. I was not sure what she meant and therefore did not answer her question.

"I was surprised that you continued to be my friend after the way I treated you," Wendy continued.

I realized that she needed reassurance from me. "Wendy, you have done so much for me since I met you. It will take a lifetime to repay you. I probably need to make a list to remind you of all your good deeds." She blushed as she looked away to hide her joy.

My friendship with Wendy was very peculiar. There was disquiet between us, and it stunted any significant growth in our relationship. We were afraid to tell each other how we truly felt, so deep feelings were never shared. When she felt that she was vulnerable after she asked me a sensitive question, she quickly retreated to her comfort zone. "Joseph, we need to get back to our studies. We have a lot to cover." It was an unfortunate way to end a meaningful conversation. There was no follow up statement from Wendy, and I did not feel the need to expose her vulnerability. We were friends who could not comfortably share our inner feelings because of fears of inadequacy. I was afraid of not measuring up to

Wendy's standards, and she was afraid of not surviving without her family's financial support. It was the last we ever spoke about our failed friendship.

Chapter 18

In late February, Francesca was chosen as the model for the front cover of a sports magazine. She received a registered mail for confirmation and a follow up telephone call. It was the happiest I had ever seen her. She beamed with a winning smile, and her beauty appeared more exotic than before. Her happiness was outwardly infectious. Although it was her success, I became transfixed in a state of exultation. It was confusing to me why the sun appeared brighter, the wind more soothing, and my taste buds enhanced. I blamed my enhanced physiological state on a unique phenomenon of inadvertent state of shared achievement, since my failures in life at that moment became irrelevant. I could not believe that a world class beauty was my love interest and closest companion.

"Who could believe that I dined with you, horsed around with you, and was fondled by you, my beauty queen?" I said to Francesca.

She smiled and playfully choked my neck. She was oblivious of the importance and the financial reward of her newfound fame. "Joseph, nothing would ever come between us. You have been good to me since we met, and I will never forget that. You gave up all you had for me. That is what I call love." Her words reassured me that our relationship would not become a casualty of her new fame and fortune.

# # #

As we waited in a local restaurant for her sorority sisters, I took time for closer physical reassessment of Francesca. The texture and color of her hair blended perfectly with her unblemished facial skin, and the rest of her body looked like a sculptured masterpiece that was draped with tight-fitting black lace. She was radiantly beautiful, and it was obvious to me that I did not fully appreciate what I had. "Joseph, why are you staring at me? Is there something wrong with my makeup?"

I smiled and hugged Francesca. "I was admiring your beauty, Fran." She was taken aback by her new name. "Fran is your new name, since most celebrities change their names after they become famous." I could tell that she was not ready to engage in an unnecessary frivolity, because her sorority sisters were walking in as I spoke.

We exchanged pleasantries with her friends before we were ushered into a private dining area in the restaurant. Her sorority sisters wore black dresses to honor one of their traditions. On rare occasions they were allowed to wear black dresses, and they felt that Francesca's success merited such an honor. Their walk to our private dining room was spectacular. It was like choreographed dance steps, as their synchronized alternating leg movements wowed the restaurant patrons.

I realized after we sat down that I was invited to what was supposed to be a private sorority dinner, because Francesca demanded my presence. Only Lisa and Wendy spoke to me after we were seated. The rest ignored me because they were not happy with Francesca's abrogation of their sorority rule. "We can't talk about menstrual cramps with him around," one of the ladies complained.

Apart from their initial complaint about me, it was a very boisterous gathering. They laughed loudly throughout our stay at the restaurant, probably out of joy that one of them would make national press.

I was not included in most of their conversation, so I stared at my food with analytical eyes. I visually dissected my steak out of boredom and pondered why my mashed potatoes were given an unnecessary central crater with a serving spoon.

"Is there something wrong with your food?" Wendy asked me.

I was not aware that she was watching me. "I was just looking at my raw steak," I said to her. I was not hungry, so I did not make any fuss about my steak, but Wendy was aware that I liked my steak well done, so she asked our waiter to return my steak to the kitchen for proper cooking.

"Wendy, when are you going to give up Joseph?" Lisa said to her. The rest of her sorority sisters asked the same question. Wendy ignored their question, but smiled mischievously. Francesca paid little attention to their comment as she discussed her upcoming trip to Jamaica for a photo shoot. The rest of the evening was filled with banter between friends.

Chapter 19

I spent less time with Francesca after she returned from Jamaica. She resorted to studying alone and never showed up for lunch at the school cafeteria. She avoided me in our physics and microbiology classes but was polite during laboratory sessions. We worked on a physics project one evening without Francesca saying a simple hello to me. I found it odd but did not ask what I had done. It was obvious that our flame had burned out. It was disheartening to me, because I was not aware that our relationship was like a light that could be switched off instantly. I tried to engage her in our usual friendly verbal jousting without any reply or rancor. She merely looked at me for less than a second without a smile or anger. I felt that I had nothing left to lose so I said, "No seductive gesture or eye contact for an old friend?"

She looked at me disapprovingly without any verbal comment. She stood up and walked away. I remained behind and finished our project.

I felt that Francesca had no further use for our friendship. No discussions or negotiations were offered to me regarding the rules of our disengagement. If she wanted a painless instant death to our relationship, she miscalculated. I was hurt more by her callous treatment than my need for explanation. In an exclusive relationship that involved mutual trust and dependency, consideration had to be given to the manner in which it was terminated.

# # #

Final examinations started in late April, but most graduating seniors were exempted if they had passing grades. Francesca had passing grades in all her classes and was therefore exempted from final examinations. There was no opportunity left for me to see her. A few days before her graduation, she wrote a note to me.

Mon Cher Joseph,

It was you who made me realize who I am and what this world has to offer a person. I'm very grateful to you for that, but, I'm more grateful to you because you're the special person in my life. My whole heart pours out to you. My body & soul feels empty without you. What can this be Joseph?? My heart is dripping tears for you, because I need you. If God meant for us to be together he will see to it that we unite into one someday. Joseph, there is something about you that has turned my heart inside out, something that words can't explain. All I know is I love you honey. I know someday when this world is lighter for us, we'll walk together under a beautiful sun that no man can ever destroy. You need to understand that just because I want to do something on my own does not mean that I will forget the old days with you. They were meaningful and challenging days that we should never forget. I'll never forget your smile and our special times together. I tried my best initially to make you happy, but I failed at the end because of my ambition. No one can imagine my pain. I was told that I have to let you go so that you would not drag my career down. My handler felt that a relationship with you is scandalous for a "supermodel" and it may affect my contract. I could not discuss it with you before now. I am ashamed of myself for selling out because of my desire to succeed. Joseph, I am tired of being poor, and could not give up an opportunity of a lifetime. I spoke to Wendy about my travails and she understood what I was going through. However, she felt that the two of us betrayed you, and the sanctity of friendship.

Remember me for who I am, and not the person they want me to be. I hope that you will find it in your heart to forgive me for the pain I may have caused you. I still plan to pay you back when I have some money.

No matter what happens, it is you that I love.

Your love

Francesca.

P.S. I only have one request; I do not want you to attend my graduation. It will be too painful to see you again.

# # #

Francesca had several speaking engagements, and invitations to fundraising events before her graduation. The summer edition of the sports magazine with Francesca's picture in the front page was available to newsstands on the first day of May. I bought a copy from the local bookstore with the intention of getting an autograph from Francesca. She became an instant celebrity and was interviewed by several national news agencies. I attended one of the events where she was an invited speaker but was not able to speak to her privately. I waited to get an autograph from her after the event, but she was prevented from speaking to me by her handlers. I stood at the spot where she shook my hand and watched as she walked away with a throng of photographers. She was not the same person I met in physics class who was in dire need to survive and succeed. She had arrived at her destination but unfortunately forgot how her trip started.

I tried to justify her actions, probably to maintain the little respect I had left for her. I stood by my mirror and asked the rational part of me a simple question. "Is it wrong to throw away a beautiful rose when it withers?" The only rational answer I had was, "It depends on the significance of the rose."

When I made it back to my apartment, I brought out my Holy Bible Catholic edition and read my favorite passage; Proverbs 30. 7-9

"I ask you, God, to let me have two things before I die: keep me from lying, and let me be neither rich nor poor. So give me only as much food as I need. If I have more, I might say that I do not need you. But if I am poor, I might steal and bring disgrace on my God."

It was gratifying to know that I had what others seek; I was neither rich nor poor, and I preserved the sanctity of friendship. I felt free for the first time since I'd started college.

CPSIA information can be obtained at www.ICGtesting.com
Printed in the USA
BVOW071857190912

300882BV00001B/15/P

9 781457 512582